S0-BOR-879

Building Towers by Rolling Dice

By Logan Rosenstein

This is a work of fiction. Names, characters, places, and incidents either are a product of the author's imagination or are used fictitiously.

Copyright © 2019 by Logan Rosenstein

All rights reserved.

ISBN: 978-1-54395-905-5

Printed in the United States of America

Edition 1.5

Preface

Over the last several years, my family and close friends have had a lot of struggles with depression, anxiety, and other common psychological stresses that have exposed a lot about them publicly. This all resulted in the loss of a significant amount of privacy that we all take for granted.

Those struggles come with a stigma that is very hard to navigate, especially for young men.

In an effort to help reduce that stigma, I wrote a book. A book that goes deep, exposing a significant amount of my personal thoughts, emotions, and struggles, which a lot of people didn't know about.

I wanted to gift them the loss of my privacy around the things they've lost. By doing this, I hope that I can reduce the stigma around what has happened to them by showing how common some of these things are amongst men from our generations.

This book tells the story of a boy named Tyler. The events and the people in this book are fictional. However, they were designed to portray my actual inner and most personal thoughts, emotions, and experiences with severe depression, anxiety, suicidal thoughts, and what it was like to go through psychotherapy and face medication options.

Every thought process Tyler has, I've had.
Every emotion Tyler feels, I've felt.
Every resulting condition Tyler has, I have had.
And the crux of every lesson learned, I've learned.

I couldn't explain thirty years of experiences that resulted in who I am today successfully in a short novel, and I wanted to do this in a way that protects certain people who influenced feelings I've had. So, I created several fake "perfect storm" situations to demonstrate how I handle and process the world around me, and fake characters who are amalgamations of a vast number of people I've interacted with in my life. These do not represent singular events or any individual person.

The events are designed in a way to hopefully make it relatable to anyone who reads this, but primarily in a way that the underlying emotions and thoughts are understood, and ultimately, to give hope in the future to him and anyone else who feels commonality between themselves and Tyler.

Logan

For Cody

Part 1

1

There is something special about high school. Maybe special isn't the right word.... Evil. There is something evil about high school. I know everyone says that and it's a cliché. But the more you think about it, the more it makes sense.

Why does this exist?

Whose idea was it to take a couple thousand kids during the most hormonal time in their lives, cram them into small classrooms, force them to get along and do group projects, and tell them they have to do everything perfectly for years or they won't get into a good college and their future will involve an apron or a delivery truck?

How is that fair? How is that right?

It feels like it's some social experiment where adults read about the great Roman Colosseum and thought, "Hey, that thing where they took all those citizens and put them into a confined space and told them compete or get eaten by lions? Let's do that, but with children."

So, there I was, standing at the top of the sand-covered underground ramp with a decorative gladiator helmet on my head blocking my visibility (*seriously, those things did not look practical*), staring at the wood gate in front of me. My eyes focused and refocused on the dust that floated through the light rays coming through the cracks in the old wooden gate beams.

The ground beneath me vibrated and pulsated from the stomps of the spectators' feet above me. Chants roared through the air, the suspense of the new meat about to enter the arena being too much for them to wait patiently for.

A man walked up from the hallway to the left of me. He handed my backpack to me and said nonchalantly, "You'll probably be fine." Shrugged his shoulders and walked off back down the dark hallway, humming some off-key version of the four tones that make up the *Hunger Games* theme song.

My heart was pounding.

The gate opened.

I took my first steps forward into the blinding light.

The stadium started chanting something different than before. It was hard to hear at first. It's strange how crowds always took a few passes at a chant before they lined up the syllables and it sounded coherent.

"Tttttttlllrrrr."

The two syllables of the word stood out as the crowd used them to find their synchronization point.

"Tttyyyyr."

The sound was so loud and fluid it completely engulfed me.

"Tyler."

"Tyler?"

Oddly sharper now, like it was coming from one person. Not a raging stadium of bloodthirsty citizens...

"Tyler Lawson?"

"What?" I said out of confusion.

I looked up from my feet, my comfort zone, to see this single voice "crowd" chanting my name. I came face-to-face with a man looking directly into my eyes. He was holding a clipboard and wearing a polo shirt that said *North Oaks High School* on his chest.

"Tyler Lawson?" he asked one more time, with his right eyebrow higher than his left.

"Yes? Yes. Here."

"Welcome back to earth," he said with a light smile, a short burst of air from his nostrils, and a hint of a grin under an attempt to stay composed.

Some laughs from all around brought me back to reality. I looked around the room to see some of my classmates clearly getting a kick out of all this.

I was sitting in a super uncomfortable high-bar-style plastic chair with metal legs at a lab table in the middle of the classroom.

My embarrassment must have been clearly visible on my face. I could feel my cheeks getting warmer. Not quite as bad as responding with "What, Mom?", something I had done in elementary school too many times, but this was still pretty bad.

"Spencer?" he continued after he looked back down at his clipboard. Looking up from his paper, he made eye contact with a kid on the other side of the room and said, "There you are." Apparently, he didn't need verbal confirmation.

At some point during my lapse in reality, I must have put my backpack on the table in front of me. Looking around the room, I saw everyone had theirs on the floor at their feet. Not wanting to stand out even more beyond my daydream spectacle, I quickly grabbed it and started to pull it toward my chest to put it down below like everyone else.

As I pulled it toward the edge of the table faster than a normal socially skilled human being would, it jolted to a stop, and my hand, gripping the bundle of canvas on its front, slipped off, slapping my thigh loudly.

A hand reached over my shoulder. Smoothly and casually, it found the bag's right shoulder strap and slowly lifted it over and free of the metal Bunsen burner nozzle in the center of the table.

"So, as I was saying, I'm Mr. Hunter. I'll be your physics teacher this year. This will be your favorite class. I'm a delight."

The room let out a laugh again, this time not directed toward me, which felt good. Mr. Hunter was smiling a bit more now as he walked over to the front of the class. He put his clipboard down on the super-long table that spanned about fifteen feet left to right between the rest of the class and the whiteboard on the front wall. It was one of those generic lab display counters complete with a sink, burner nozzles, beakers, computer, and piles of papers.

Reaching into a drawer on the far side, he pulled out a small remote. Aiming it at the projector mounted on the ceiling above my table, he pushed a button.

Nothing.

He pushed it again, a little more forcibly, the remote's aim clearly dipping down from his thumb's excessive downward pressure.... Nothing.

"Of course. Batteries would be nice," he said, a little frustrated.

"Tyler, can you please jump up there and hit the power button?"

Shit. He said my name again. Immediately my stomach tightened as my diaphragm dropped to the floor inside my body. Air flooded in through my nose with an audible hiss. With my eyes darting around nervously, trying not to make eye contact with the other people at my table, I climbed up to the place where my backpack had rested a minute before.

Reaching up above my head, I pressed what I assumed was the on/off button. The label on the button was worn off after what must have been hundreds of manual presses. He really needed to buy some batteries....

The fans on the sides of the projector spun to life and the light next to the button I pressed started blinking green.

4

"Perfect. Thanks, Tyler. Be careful getting down please."

Turning back around, Mr. Hunter reached up and pulled a string down, rolling out a white projector screen from its case mounted above the whiteboard until it maxed out, clicked, and stayed in place after rolling back up a few inches.

As the projector started to warm up, Mr. Hunter's computer desktop, completely covered from corner to corner with icons, started to slowly come into view on the projector screen in front of us. This guy needed to learn how to use folders. That many disorganized icons would stress me out.

He walked over to his computer at the far right of the long table. After a few clicks of the mouse, a presentation took over the screen.

North Oaks High School
Mr. Hunter
Physics I

"I'm going to be real for a second. This is going to be the most important class you will ever take in your life. Not because of the physics but because I'm teaching it."

The class laughed again. He didn't seem to have a smile anymore. Was he being serious right now? He was pretty full of himself. Was that a joke?

"First things first…" With the remote clearly out of batteries, he reached down to the keyboard and loudly clicked the space bar, moving the presentation slides forward. A white slide with big, black, bold letters said:

I know when you're texting.
No one looks down at their crotch every 90
seconds and giggles.

"I have a policy starting immediately after I finish this sentence. Anyone caught texting during my class has to read the texts out loud to the rest of the class. Then, you will have to take a selfie with me, text the image to your parents, and post it to social media. Which social media site? I get to choose."

The class didn't laugh at that one. There was a bit of rustling as people tried to casually slide their phones back into their pockets.

"In case you were curious, this is a science class. Science classes have experiments and projects. Therefore, you will have to work with other people. I know, it sucks. But you will have to deal with it. The seating assignment in this class was done entirely at random. I definitely didn't call your old teachers and ask who to keep separate from each other… maybe."

When he clicked his keyboard, the next slide popped up on the screen, showing a top-down map of the room, complete with desks and littered with names.

"Here are the seating assignments for the first half of the year. Find your name, and please move over to the seat you are assigned to."

Everyone squinted at the screen because Mr. Hunter clearly didn't take the time to properly focus the projector, making all the fine-print names look like gibberish after the capital first letters of everyone's first and last names. One by one, everyone found their initials on the screen and they started to grab their bags off the ground and walk over to their new homes.

I was lucky and only had to move over a few chairs at the same table, but most people had to make big moves. This was clearly frustrating to some as they moved to opposite ends of the room from their friends they'd deliberately sat next to when they first walked in.

Mr. Hunter clearly had done his research.

A boy wearing a loose-fitting T-shirt, shorts, and skate shoes pulled my old stool out and sat down on it. His hair was unruly, dried out, and bleached about halfway through each strand. Brown at the base, yellow at the end.

I knew what that meant. Chlorine.

"Do you swim?" I asked.

"Yeah, I play on the JV water polo team here," he said with some pride.

"You do? I played in a club, and my brother played at his school back in Southern California. We're supposed to come to practice today to meet the coach and try to get on the team."

Because I'd always kept my hair short and straight, it never had the chance to bleach out like his did before I cut it off, so he probably didn't know I swam until I mentioned it. I figured trying to force some conversation was a good "social" thing to do. I was new at this school and didn't want to be the creepy silent kid in the corner people thought ate paint chips.

"Meet the coach? You just did," he said with a chuckle.

"What? No. Mr. Hunter?"

"Yup. I must say, you made one hell of a first impression. 'Tyler? Tyler? Tyler...' Ha-ha. I wish I had a video of it."

Shit.

He must have seen the reaction on my face because he followed up by saying, "It's okay, he's cool. I'm Spencer, by the way."

"Tyler."

With a nod and a small smile, he said, "I know."

"Right."

Great way to start all this out, Tyler.

From the front of the classroom, Mr. Hunter flipped to the next slide in his presentation. A picture of a star exploding appeared on the screen. It looked like a computer graphic, but it looked pretty detailed, making me question if it was real or not. Rings of what I assumed were gas and flames shot out to the right and left, like two short wineglasses glued together at their base. But you couldn't have flames in space, right? A tiny dot in the center shone bright white like someone had spilled a white paint drop on the picture.

Mr. Hunter walked over to the classroom door and flipped a few switches, which turned off all the lights in the room. After he did that, the image seemed to change. The entire screen was filled with little pink, orange, blue, and white dots of all sizes and brightness.

It was beautiful.

He must have deliberately blurred the seating chart to mess with us because this was in near-perfect focus.

The room was silent now, looking at the screen.

"Pretty cool, huh?" he said casually.

"This is a picture taken by the Hubble Space Telescope of Supernova 1987A, or SN 1987A for short, surrounded by the Large Magellanic Cloud galaxy.

"A supernova is the last stage in a star's life, where it makes its final mark on the universe with a massive and world-shattering explosion that causes its material, and that of whatever was unfortunate enough to live nearby, to fly across the galaxy. That material flies for light-years until it either crashes into another star or planet after getting caught in its gravity or it just keeps floating off into eternity."

He paused for a minute, clearly hoping this dramatic story would shock and awe his new students. Looking around the room, it was clear this was high school. So, half of the class was already struggling to care, and the other half looked at Mr. Hunter with a transparent *So? I threw an M80 into a fire pit while camping once* look on their faces.

I've always been a fan of space and science. Curious what he would say next, I looked back to him.

"As the name suggests, it was seen here on earth in 1987. But that isn't when the actual blue supergiant star exploded. This star was 168,000 light-years away from earth, which means that the visible light thrown out in every direction during the explosion took about 168 *thousand* years to reach earth before we could even see this."

He emphasized the *thousand* so hard his geek flag was flying high for the whole class to see.

"By the time we were able to see the light from the explosion, the star and all its explosive glory was long gone, dead for the better part of 175 millennia.

"When the star began to collapse, before the visible explosion took place, little fermion particles called neutrinos shot outwards in all directions. Observatories here on earth were actually able to record about twenty-five of these particles reaching earth just two or three hours before any visible light from the explosion could be seen.

"Think about that for a second.... Evolved apes were able to measure a handful of individual particles from a star too small to be visible to your naked eye, so far away that it would take you 168,000 years traveling at the speed of light just to get there.

"Not only that, but for humans to understand that this was connected to a galactic event so catastrophically massive and far away is a mind-blowing concept on its own."

Mr. Hunter paused to look around the room again, to see how many students he'd lost from what he probably felt was a Shakespearean-level performance. Surprised that most of the class seemed to at least have their bodies turned toward the front of the class, he continued.

"Physics is the study of everything. From the makeup of the individual neutrino particles to the forces and resulting conditions of a star gone supernova. Studying how things too small for the dusty microscopes in the corner of the room to see and things tens to hundreds of times larger than our own sun and beyond are made and behave, and how the rules of our universe control how they interact with each other... physics."

He'd clearly rehearsed this, because after the room sat in silence for about four seconds, digesting what he said, the bell rang, signaling the end of class. As everyone started to pack their bags and hustle out of the room, Mr. Hunter said loudly over the noise and in a hurry, "I want you all to read Stephen Hawking's 1966 doctoral thesis on the properties of an expanding universe and bring notes on what he got wrong for class tomorrow."

Funny.

Spencer grabbed his backpack from off the floor and swung it over his shoulder effortlessly. It just hung there so lightly with a small weight at the bottom. Like it had nothing but a brown paper lunch bag with a Coke can and a peanut butter sandwich in it. No books. No binders. Casual.

Not like me.

Not having all the essentials with me would stress me out. I like to be prepared. I was the guy that people bugged when they needed something because they knew my backpack was the Mary Poppins handbag of "junk."

They called it junk. But it was only junk when they didn't need it. When it was needed, it was pure gold.

Color-coded binder tabs, six pens (two of each color: black, blue, and red), highlighters in three colors for different topics, four number-two pencils (two mechanical with replacement lead and erasers and two traditional with mini sharpener), graphing calculator with replacement batteries, hand sanitizer, and flushable wet wipes.

Gotta love that irritable bowel syndrome, exacerbated by stress. A new school, in a new town, with new people? Yeah, I was stressed.

I was prepared.

"See you at practice?" Spencer asked over his shoulder as he started to walk toward the door.

"Yeah, if I survive the rest of the day."

"You'll be fine," he said with a slight laugh. "This place is pretty harmless."

I wish I could have that mentality. Nothing was harmless.

2

At two thirty, when the last period of the day ended, I made my way to my locker in the hallway outside of Mr. Hunter's classroom. The school had an open feel, where a bunch of buildings that housed the classrooms were connected by outdoor walkways.

Trees lined every path and it was clear this school had a healthy landscaping budget. It felt more like a private school than a public one. At my last school, they barely had enough money for gym equipment. Let's just say they weren't concerned with the gardening.

It was refreshing.

Throughout the day, I had this feeling of claustrophobia. I'm not a claustrophobic person, really. It was just like all these classes and all these people made me feel a little cramped.

The trees and the air didn't seem to be important to anyone else. This place was like one of those newspapers run by old people talking about how kids these days never looked up from their phones. Everyone was walking around face down, phone screens up.

Going outside between classes seemed to help me breathe. Literally. I guess I was holding my breath all day, because I felt totally different when I walked through those doors to the outdoor walkways.

It was like the feeling when you got out of a car after a long drive to the snow. After breathing in the recirculating warm air in the car for hours, the car stopped. You grabbed the junk lying around you and threw it in your bag, then grabbed the handle to open the door. The instant that door opened even a small crack, you could feel the cool air hit your face, forcing you to take a deep breath. With the cold air filling your lungs, it just felt like it was "real" air. Not the "fake" air that you couldn't feel when you breathed normally. Yes, it kept you alive, but you didn't feel like it was doing anything special for you. This air slowed your breathing and just made you feel refreshed.

After dealing with all the fake air all day, I needed a moment to just stand there and breathe.

The image that hits you about this is probably from those allergy medication TV commercials where someone sneezes and takes a pill, then all of a sudden, they are on top of a mountain taking deep breaths. That's a bit too scripted.

It was more like those horribly acted infomercials where it was a black-and-white video of someone scratching and itching in a sweater harder and more aggressively than anyone not on cocaine or bath salts would. When they took off the sweater, the world turned into color, and the person fell to a comfortable beanbag chair and smiled.

No, that analogy wasn't breathing, but that's how it felt in my brain.

Freedom from the itch...

Throwing the books that I didn't need for the night's homework into my locker felt good, too. The less I needed to worry about tonight, the better. But I'll admit it, *throwing* was a strong word for what I did. My locker was clean. I placed the books in order of class period so I could grab them in order from left to right the next day between classes. I always hated messy lockers. Why would you deliberately set yourself up to lose things or need to dig to find what you need? It was just easier to have things ready to go.

Resting on top of my books was a small drawstring bag with a yellow water polo ball logo on the front of it and the words *SoCal Water Polo Club* encircling it.

I grabbed it and threw it over my right shoulder alongside by backpack and started the walk down to the pool deck. It was a new addition to the school after some wealthy former student donated it because his kids wanted to play water polo here.

Must be nice to be able to throw a few million bucks around like that.

Rounding the corner to the pool entrance, I found my brother, Luke, waiting for me with a few other guys who looked like seniors on the polo team.

Luke was a senior. He was on varsity as a junior back at his high school in Southern California and was one of the best hole sets in the league.

Hole set was the hardest position in the game. You had to fight the hardest, act the fastest, and be able to monitor all the other players in the half circle around you in order to make quick plays without accidentally giving the ball to the other team.

You had to be aggressive, but not aggressive enough to get a foul called. It required a sort of composure most guys couldn't do. How did you wrestle with someone who wanted to drown you for a half hour and not get frustrated enough to just hit him?

It was an art form. Luke was Leonardo da Vinci. When I played that position, I was finger-painting with two colors because the teachers were too afraid I'd make a mess with a third.

But that was Luke, the best at what he did and calm as shit when he did it.

"Tyler. You lived," he said with a chuckle as I walked up to him.

"I guess," I said with a hint of embarrassment. It was always fun to get introduced to strangers as the guy who had questionable fortitude.

"Guys, this is my brother, Tyler."

"Hey," one of them said without much expression.

"I'll see you guys in the pool. Tyler and I need to go talk to Coach." Luke clearly noticed that the guys weren't that interested in meeting a small freshman and dismissed them.

He was good at that. I don't know how he knew what was going through people's heads sometimes, but nevertheless, he knew. He could read the most minute social cue so fast, and act appropriately to keep the room level.

Most people might not see those cues, or act to protect other people when they did. They'd probably think how to protect themselves. He never seemed to do that. He seemed to include me in his plans to handle the situation, and always made me feel like I was supposed to be there.

Someone doesn't want to be around my brother and me? It's cool, they can leave if they want was how I imagined it going through his head. Not aggressive for showing disinterest or disrespect. Just casual dismissal from the situation.

No one left upset.

Luke turned and started walking toward Mr. Hunter, who, after changing out of his khakis and polo shirt into board shorts, T-shirt, flip-flop sandals, and a wide-brim straw beach hat, looked like a totally different human being.

I followed Luke as we approached him, and he turned to face Luke and me with a welcoming face and said, "Hi, Tyler. And you must be Luke," as he reached out toward Luke for a strong handshake.

"Normally, our team has an extensive tryout phase followed by hell week in the middle of August. But since you guys just moved into town, I took the liberty of reaching out to your old coaches and got their input instead."

Damn, this guy liked to do his research.

"Luke, go ahead and get suited up and I'll introduce you to the varsity team before they get in."

"Will do." Luke gave me a slap on the back as he walked off to the guys he'd been talking to when I showed up at the pool. They were already starting to deck change.

"Tyler, I think you may be JV material, but I'd like to see how you play with our freshman team first. The goalies on the two teams all practice together, swapping in and out so they get practice defending against a wider variety of players. So, you'll practice at the same time as JV after varsity finishes up around four o'clock. Warm-up starts at three thirty in the small pool, so suit up and stretch for a bit before then."

Deck changing is where you threw your towel around your waist and you awkwardly fumbled around as one hand took your pants and underwear off before pulling your suit on, all while your other hand held on for dear life to the towel so you didn't end up exposing yourself to a pool deck filled with people. After a while, it became second nature. For most people...

Luke was used to it because his old school allowed it. But the club I played for had a strong rule against it since we practiced at the same time as the girls' team. To keep things from getting "complicated" from a weak towel grip, they had us all either arrive at practice with the suit on under our clothes or use the locker rooms.

So, needless to say, I had one more awkward thing to worry about today.

Great.

"Mr. Hunter, where are the rest of the JV and freshman players? This looks like it's just varsity," I asked, looking around the deck, not recognizing anyone my age.

"Since they start a little later, they like to mess around on campus or walk down to the strip mall a few blocks away and grab some food before practice. They will be back soon to get ready," he said.

"But since you're new, I'd recommend you stay here and watch varsity practice to get acclimated to the team and our training style a bit before you get in the pool.

"Also, on the deck, I'm Coach. Mr. Hunter is gone as soon as the massive ugly hat gets put on." Again, that smile. Very welcoming and not judgmental. I liked him.

"Sounds good, Coach."

As he turned back to face the pool, he asked a couple of varsity guys near him to put the goals in. After finishing deck changing, two guys picked up the floating goals from the pool deck and slid them into the water and connected the lane lines, the cables that lined four sides of the rectangle perimeter of the play area, to the walls securing it.

I walked over to the bleachers to sit and watch the practice. The first time all day that I could sit alone and not have to socialize and talk to people… It felt good. I felt I could finally start to catch my breath and begin to recover from the constant state of discomfort I'd had all day.

Curious what was happening with my friends back at my old school, I pulled out my phone and opened one of the half dozen social media apps I had. I almost never posted, but I still had an account so that I could see what my friends were up to. Now, with the distance, it was the only way for me to know what was happening. I hated phone calls, so this was a perfect way to stay connected. Quick pictures or videos with some text every once in a while.

Today was their first day of high school too, so the main feed was covered with pictures of Luke's old school. I recognized some of the places behind the awkward facial expressions plastered in the front of the selfie, but it was hard to picture all of it.

They all looked like they were having fun. I guess their first day was going more smoothly than mine.

Just to let them know I was alive, I lifted my phone up and took a picture of the pool deck from the bleachers. Bright sun, new pool, light blue waters…

After I clicked post, the image slipped into the top of the main feed above all the others my friends were making.

I should probably follow Spencer. Show people that I made at least one friend today. Realizing I had no idea what Spencer's last name was, it proved to be a failed attempt. Could I claim a friend if I didn't know his last name?

Instantly, I was reminded that I was still alone in a new place.

I hated new things. Familiarity was comfort. New surroundings, new people, new responsibilities... stress. I was always able to handle things, and I wasn't failing at anything, really. But I was never comfortable doing them.

Maybe that's why I was a goalie when I played water polo. Field positions like point and hole set had variability. Unpredictable situations caused by the other team that you had to read and adapt to with a full 360-degree perspective.

Yes, in the field you had offensive plays that you rehearsed and could perform like it was second nature. But, since you didn't know the other team's plays, on defense it was a gamble most of the time.

Goalie was a defense position, but not in the same sense. While the field players dealt with that variability, I was in a fixed position that had somewhat standard responses to predictable situations.

To me, it was about geometry and logic.

They had a ball they needed to get behind me. I had a fixed position to operate in. So, I had to put my body directly between the person with the ball and the objective behind me.

If I had a goal that was an upright rectangle, and the players facing it only had, at most, 180 degrees to work with, all I had to do was figure out which degree to focus on. The wider the shooter was from front and center, the sharper the angle was and the smaller the goal was for them, now a trapezoid. So, ninety-nine percent of the time, I only had to work with about 120 to 140 degrees.

The highest variability zone was a shot from directly in front of me since the target was the largest for the player with the ball, and I had to figure out if I had to move left, right, or stay in the middle. In that situation, I would monitor the eyes of the shooter, the arm angle, and when he began to throw, the trajectory of the lower arm holding the ball. If I was focused, that would tell me all I needed to know.

It was even easier if he were positioned to either side of center. I did the math, and with my wingspan, I could cover the whole goal without having to decide to go left or right if he was shooting from the 0-70 or the 110-180-degree zones. Which, given the six-man offensive structure of a rectangle where they set themselves in the corners of the rectangle, with the two remaining guys in the center point of the long sides of the rectangle directly in front of the goal, I had four out of six people in my zones of minimal variability.

Those were good odds when I needed to predict where to move my body.

For four of them, I slid slightly toward them, cutting off their angle and reducing my need to lunge. And for two of them, I only needed to worry about the farthest guy in the center the most. The hole set, the position Luke played, was the closest position to the goalie and rarely shot. Most of the time, in my experience, they drew a foul and passed quickly to another player who fired off a quick shot at the goal. When hole sets did shoot, it was aggressive, fast, and hurt because it was usually at face level. But at that angle, I could usually reduce their left-to-right field by moving toward them. I was no longer at the base of their shooting triangle but moving toward the top point, where the left-to-right distance of the triangle was shortest and my wingspan could cover.

Yeah, I over-mathed athletics. I never told the other players because most other athletes didn't seem to want to think of their teammates using math and not their innate "athletic skill."

No math or geeks allowed. It was one more thing that made me different, so it didn't make sense to surface deliberately. I had a hard enough time fitting in. It was safer in my head than on my tongue.

It seemed like the athletes who started at super-young ages, long before they were taking geometry or physics in school, were hardwired to think, "If I do *this*, then *that* will happen," learning through cause and effect.

When you saw the toddler try to hit the baseball off the tee, he wasn't thinking, *If I hit the ball at rest at a twenty degree upward trajectory with a bat where the point of contact is aligned along the lengthwise centerline farthest from the hand grip, I will get maximum impact force of ten thousand Newtons exerted on the ball where the resulting trajectory will place it to the left field equidistant between the center and left fielder, giving me the best chance at a double.*

They either had a coach or a parent guiding them to the ideal result, sometimes without full explanation why.

"Swing like this."

They learned *I did this before and it worked. Let me keep doing it that way, making minor changes here and there to see if I can improve.*

When they got older, many seemed less focused on figuring out why something worked and more interested in what they already knew. If they were good, they would try to alter what they already knew and improve.

At the end of the day, I got that this process was basically the same thing as science. Observe something, see if it could be repeated or improve it under the same conditions, and find out *why* it did what it did that consistently.

But ignoring that third part of that process seemed pretty universal in amateur athletics. It seemed to be that unspoken thing athletes had with each other. Either believe it was their unique human capability and that science and math were irrelevant, or they used math and science without saying it out loud.

Yes, I was in little league. I played basketball, baseball, soccer, water polo, as well as half a dozen other things growing up. But I never trusted coaches. I don't know why, I just never trusted them. If they were so great, why weren't they pros? Why were they teaching a dozen eight-year-olds how to kick a ball instead of making millions in front of millions?

I listened to what they said, but I questioned everything. Why would I do it that way? Why did it work when I did this? If it worked for them, why would it work for me? If I changed it a bit for me, would it work better than it did for them?

When I was little, I rarely had those answers. But it didn't stop me from obsessing about that one word...

Why?

In classes, I always secretly laughed at the football players who would say things like "Why do I need to learn [insert anything]? I'm not going to need it when I play in college or for the NFL." Then, they went to practice and kneeled while watching their coach outline a new play that used angles, velocity, parabolic trajectories, psychology, and physiology hidden behind Xs, Os, and lines.

Or my favorite, they would watch the NFL Combine on TV, where college athletes performed athletic feats in the hopes of making the draft, and witnessed state-of-the-art technology measuring thousands to millions of data points used to determine athletic potential.

What did they think those sensors in the shoes were measuring when they ran?

Why were all those cameras monitoring the QB's throwing arm from a full 360-degree perspective?

Why was the obstacle course configured in that specific way, making athletes' bodies twist and turn in ways that would make a contortionist feel at home?

Sports used this shit all the time, whether people realized it or not.

I didn't mean this in an *I'm better and smarter than you* sort of way. I honestly didn't think that I was smarter. I was just different. I seemed to think differently than other people. If anyone saw half the shit that passed through my brain, they'd think I needed a helmet and someone to cut my food into small pieces for me. Not a Nobel Prize.

Different isn't smarter or better, it's just different.

Some of the best athletes in the world do all the math, logical processing, and physics in their head without even realizing it. It's just "what they do."

To me, that was more impressive than having to calculate everything consciously all the time. I just didn't get why people had to pretend like it wasn't a factor in why they were as good as they were.

Luke was kind of like that. Not the *aggressively against math, science and the rest* part. He was an excellent student. But he never seemed to bring it into sports or anything else. Or at least outwardly. He was just naturally good at them. Subconsciously, he must just have done the calculations and acted on them appropriately, without the standard fifteen presses of the "clear" button on the calculator between each decision that I had to do.

Who knows? Maybe he did it like I did and just hid it well. But I doubted that. He wasn't as neurotic as I was.

I sat there for an hour and watched Luke swim circles around the team as they scrimmaged. He was too good at this. He made a few goals with well-executed backhand shots, set up countless players with perfectly placed assist passes, and was that perfect balance of aggressive yet appropriate.

It was his first time in the pool with these guys, and he was already in the team. Not from an official position, although I was sure Coach would make that happen, but from a cohesion perspective.

He was in.

3

About ten minutes before I had planned to change and stretch, a group of guys walked through the entrance to the pool. They all seemed to have heard the guy in the front say something funny because most of them were laughing at something he said, and he had a pretty devious grin on his face.

I wondered what he'd said.

In the middle of the group, I saw Spencer from Mr. Hunter's class. And like his preparedness in class, he had the bare minimum.

There was a tiny hotel-size towel over one shoulder, probably stolen at an away tournament after forgetting to bring a towel from home, and now it was his nostalgic memorabilia taking its place in his daily social routine. He also had a pair of goggles and a Speedo hanging over his shoulder, the towel passing through one of the legs of his suit and the goggles' head strap, holding them in place.

No bag for sunscreen, spare suits, eardrops to get the water out after practice, water bottle, an extra set of goggles in case his leaked or the rubber strap broke…

Nothing extra.

They all made their way over to one of the far corners of the deck. Probably to prevent Coach from eavesdropping on their conversations.

I took that opportunity to start deck changing and prepping for practice. Wrapping my towel around me and holding it in place with my left hand, I reached underneath it with my right and began unbuckling my belt and taking off my pants.

As my zipper dropped, belt and button undone, the fly flopped open and the waist tension eased. This next part of dropping my pants, complete with my loose boxers, down to my ankles was the riskiest. So, I looked up to see if anyone was watching me before making the plunge down.

Looking over at the group of guys Spencer had walked in with, I noticed they were starting to get dressed too. I made eye contact with Spencer. He threw his chin up toward the air with two raised eyebrows and threw an arm up, waving me over to come join him and the rest of the group.

Right now? Should I finish suiting up first?

He must have seen me struggle with my decision, and just waved at me a second time to come over.

Okay, right now. Did I leave my bag and stuff or bring it? *You're overthinking this, Tyler.*

Just bring it all over there.

I threw my backpack over my shoulder and grabbed my water polo bag with my right hand. And with my left hand holding my towel in place, I started to walk over toward Spencer.

About halfway there, I started to feel my pants begin to make their journey south without my express permission. Both my hands were occupied, so I couldn't reach down to hold them up. My walk slowly transitioned into a waddle as my stance became wider and wider, hoping that the wider the V of my legs, the lower the probability my pants would fall farther.

I was wrong. I forgot that the towel was tighter around my legs than it should have been because of my fear of it falling. It couldn't be let out a bit, having only one hand to perform the maneuver. And being so tight on the sides of my legs in waddle form told me, "Sorry, dude, this is as wide as it gets...." You'd think the pressure from the tight towel would hold the pants in place, but the motion as I walked forward give it a soft shimmy, preventing it from staying secure.

Shit.

Only twenty feet left to go. Hold it together, Tyler.

Fuck, I had to go down more stairs to get out of the bleachers to the deck...

Slowly taking baby steps down the steps, I made it to the bottom safely but must have looked like an idiot.

Ten feet. I can do this...

Approaching Spencer, I tried to act like there was nothing weird going on and said, "Hey, what's up?"

"That was quite the trek you just made," Spencer said with a little chuckle.

"Ha... yeah," I responded, looking down along my towel toward my feet.

"Hey, guys," Spencer said, addressing the larger group. "This is Tyler. He's in my science class with Coach." And with a hint of sarcasm he continued... "If he's good enough, he might play with us this season..."

I put my bags down on the floor.

At that exact moment, like a classic sketch comedy show, my backpack, overweight from my junk, slid down my body, making contact with my towel. The towel broke loose from my left hand and fell, right along with my pants and underwear. With a loud clunk, my metal belt buckle hit the concrete as my pants hit the ground.

And... that's my dick.

If they hadn't been paying attention to Spencer's introduction of me, they sure as hell were now.

Did you ever have those dreams of going up to do a class presentation and realizing you were in your underwear? You know the feeling when a hot girl told you that your fly was down after a half hour of trying to impress her?

You know, the feeling you had when your entire future seemed instantly fucked? When you knew it was your fault, and the classic record scratch halt you saw in '90s comedies didn't do this feeling justice?

Enough analogies? Get the idea? Yeah, this was *way* worse than all of those...

I felt like a sledgehammer hit my chest, forcing the air out of every inch of my body. My brain instantly screamed like I was on a roller coaster about to make the big drop, and I realized that very second that my seat belt wasn't locked....

You might be thinking, "Isn't this water polo, the sport where you deliberately wear a skimpy Speedo? This isn't exactly a huge step away from the norm in terms of exposure..."

Let me explain something.

Fourteen years old wasn't exactly the age where you were at your peak physical development yet. And on top of that, everyone around you had seen enough porn to think *they knew* what a dick size was supposed to be. It didn't matter that these guys didn't do the comparison of their own dicks to this unrealistic standard, realizing it was bullshit. No, their brains instantly tied developmentally appropriate genitalia to metaphors like *Dude, when you're having sex, it must feel like throwing a hot dog down a hallway*, or *Do you hear the splash when you drop your pencil down a well?*

Speedos left a surprising amount to the imagination. For instance, when you wore two at the same time, the vacuum-seal appearance was gone, and you had a more undiscernible bulge. You could also tuck your junk every which way to give the appearance of... structure... when there weren't a ton of bricks in the foundation...

Without them... you were flying free, for all eyes to see....

I scrambled to reach down and pull up my towel, but the deed was done.

After a few seconds of silence, Spencer did his light chuckle and said, "Well, that went well. You have a way of making first impressions, Tyler." A few others laughed and shook their heads, still smiling.

Just like class earlier that same day, I felt my face heat up from blushing. My eyes started darting around the ground and were probably the size of bowling balls.

Seeing my reaction, Spencer joked, "That was way worse than you think it was. But don't worry. We will probably forget this when we all die."

He slapped me on the back with a friendly hit and got back to putting his own suit on.

The rest of the group did the same. And in expert fashion, they were all dressed without reproductive organ exposure in about sixty seconds.

"If you're going to play with us, you'd better be a better water polo player than you are at deck changing," one of the guys to my right said.

He was about my height, five feet four or five inches, but was ridiculously skinny. Probably a good thirty pounds less than me. He had a half-serious look on his face mixed with a bit of cockiness.

I didn't say anything, no need to try to puff up my chest or make waves. Since I'd missed hell week, their boot-camp-style training session during the summer, they probably felt I didn't deserve to be there. *A team that suffers together, wins together.* That was the super-basic coach cliché my old coach used to say as validation for abuse. I hadn't suffered with these guys yet, so I wouldn't win with them yet either.

I'd have to show them I could play, not tell them.

Spencer, now fully suited up, looked over at the guy who spoke and said, "Hey, Brandon. You remember that time your suit was torn off playing set in a scrimmage during hell week? You ended up skinny-dipping over to the side of the pool where the girls' team was sitting, and you had to ask one of them to bring you a spare from your bag? What was it that Emily said? I think it was 'The pool heater must be broken again.'"

Everyone laughed, except Brandon, now fuming.

"Dude, JKYS," Brandon said to Spencer. I had no idea what that meant, but Spencer smiled and gave him the middle finger.

I tried not to laugh, but I couldn't help but break a small smile. More from appreciation for what Spencer did than the joke itself. But either way, Brandon saw it and didn't like it.

Everyone stretched a little bit, swinging their arms every which way, and jumped into the little pool to start warming up. Warm-ups were pretty universal from team to team, so there were no issues there following along. A few laps here and there, some eggbeater leg work, treading back and forth, etc. And as usual, there was a guy or two pretending to fix their goggles in an effort to avoid exercise.

No matter how many teams I'd seen and played with, the tactics people used to avoid work never changed. We all thought we were clever, but I'm sure every coach knew what was up.

There was something about being in a pool that just relaxed my mind. All the stress of the day and the catastrophic mishaps I managed to pull off were momentarily gone as the rest of the guys swam their laps and didn't talk to me.

I hated swimming laps. It was boring and was too much time to spend in my head. But being in pools with a casual warm-up agenda and no conversation was the best.

Varsity was just finishing up as I started to get too comfortable and forgot why I was in the pool to begin with. Luke and the rest of varsity jumped out of the pool. I say jumped because it always looked like they literally jumped.

Like a sea lion breaching out of the water at forty miles an hour to smoothly land on the floating dock to get some sun.

Most pools for polo and swim teams weren't like your normal community or backyard pool. The deck was about twelve inches above the waterline. This was because there was often a small cavern built into the wall at the water level that lined the entire perimeter of the pool. Water flowed from the surface of the pool over the edge into this belowdeck channel, directing the water flow into the drains, which fed the extensive filtration systems.

The filtration needed for a pool like this had to be insane. I'm sure that it said in the manual somewhere, *Due to the gallons per hour of water requiring filtration and chemical dissemination as a result of regular rotations of people in a pool at maximum capacity, this system is designed to remove sunscreen oils that wash off swimmers in an aquatic environment, along with* other contaminants.

Let's be honest, we all know what *other contaminants* means. Have you ever wondered why swim and water polo teams don't take a lot of bathroom breaks to run off to the locker room? Spencer's hair was bleaching from excessive chlorine exposure. Chlorine was used not to prevent algae growth. I'm sure that was just the secondary benefit after *neutralization and sanitation of other contaminants.*

Anyway... with the pool floor being a minimum of seven feet below the waterline, I knew the varsity players weren't using the ground to push off. It was all upper body. They just put both hands on the deck above head level and in one smooth move threw their bodies upwards like doing a pull-up, but with enough force to bring their entire upper body high enough out of the water for their arms to lock straight. Supporting their body up, deck now at waist level and water mid-thigh, they just swung a knee up easily and stepped out of the pool.

Smooth.

Freshmen often didn't have the muscles to do this in one move yet, probably because of a mix of puberty in its early stages along with not having four years of hell week and protein powders in their system. We still fumbled a little bit.

But varsity was smooth...

As the rest of varsity got out of the pool, they all started circling Coach. I couldn't hear what he was saying, he was too far away, but I could guess what it was. After he finished speaking, a few of the guys gave Luke an audible smack on the back and Coach shook his hand.

He was on the team.

As everyone turned and walked back to dry off and change back into their clothes, Luke looked over to the small pool and found me looking at him. He smiled back and nodded.

Coach was walking over to the small pool now. The guys who were "fixing their goggles" miraculously fixed them that very second and pushed off the wall to swim a quick lap now that he was watching.

"Okay, guys, time to switch pools," he said and turned back toward the main pool.

Before walking away, he did a casual about-face and said, "Nick and Chris, now that your goggles are fixed, you can fix the warm-up pool tarps."

Confirmed. Coaches knew the tricks.

"Oh, yeah, for the next activity, too, we won't be needing the goals just yet, so can you please unhook them and move them to the sides of the pool, out of the main swim lanes? Thanks."

The two guys, having been caught red-handed, sulked over to the far end of the warm-up pool and began pulling the long and heavy blue tarps off their storage rollers and over the surface of the pool. They were used to keep the heat trapped underneath, reducing the energy costs to maintain the pool temp when it wasn't being used.

For something designed for energy efficiency, they seemed to take an awful lot of energy to use…

As they pulled the tarps, the rest of us walked over and casually jumped into the main pool. Varsity hadn't cleaned up the balls they'd used in their scrimmage. So, naturally the nearest guys grabbed them and immediately began passing them around to each other.

With a loud laugh, Coach walked to the edge of the deck and had everyone throw the balls out of the pool and onto the deck.

"Did you seriously think we would just start practice without a little work first? Everyone out of the water. If you think I'm going to be so easy you could just get straight to it without some pain, you don't know me very well."

There were about thirty of us between freshmen and JV, so Coach had us all line up on the deck, aimed at the normal swim lanes, about four guys per lane.

"It's time to get some blood flowing to your arms and legs. I trust you had a quality warm-up, so this shouldn't hurt too much," he said sarcastically.

"Today, we are going to start with some swim and eggbeater in-and-outs. Here are the rules. No diving. No touching the sides of the pool except to pull yourself out for the land-based parts. On my whistle, one by one, you will jump feet first into the pool. Without pushing off the walls, you are to swim head up to the other end of the pool and pull yourself out onto the deck. Once up there, do ten pushups and line back up. Again, on my whistle, one by one you are to jump back into the pool feet first. No diving, no pushing off the wall. Then, with eggbeater, tread your way back to this side of the pool with your wrists out of the water the whole way. If your hands get wet, swim back to the wall and start over. When you finally make it back to this side of the pool, pull yourself out and do ten sit-ups.

"Then, you guessed it, line back up. Wash, rinse, and repeat. I'll tell you when you're done. No need to keep count. I'll take care of it."

Every guy was running through the exercise in their heads, trying to find a way to make it easier or cheat it. But it was clear that Coach had thought this through. No diving or pushing off the wall; those were tools used to reduce the distance you needed to swim. We were swimming head up so we didn't need goggles, so, no opportunity to "fix" them. Everyone waited for his whistle to start each round and he didn't say how many we were going to do, so no opportunity to pretend like you lapped someone or miscount the laps to finish early.

It was going to be painful.

Coach was smiling.

Maybe this guy I thought was kind and nerdy was actually sadistic…

He put the plastic whistle to his lips and let it rip. The first row of guys jumped in feet first and began swimming. I was fourth in my lane, so on the last whistle, I jumped in and set off to the far end.

I don't know if you've ever done an exercise like this before, but as bad as it sounded, it was even worse in reality. Yes, the predictable stuff happened, your arms, chest, thighs, and abs start burning from being used at every step. But it was for reasons you probably didn't think about. It was the dizziness and minor delirium that set in.

With normal exercise, your body stayed in one orientation. Lying down to swim, standing up to run… So, your heart had a somewhat fixed pressure to keep your blood at. Going from lying down swimming to standing on the deck, to sit-up crunches and upright treading, your body was always having to adjust how it pumped your blood. It was like going from lying down at the dentist and trying to stand up too fast, making you dizzy from the low pressure in your brain…

But you needed to do this over and over and over again...

Also, in normal exercises, you could do a normal breathing cycle. In your mouth, out your nose, steady pace, and so on. With this workout, it was interrupted in every phase. Jump in, hold your breath for a few seconds. Swim across breathing entirely through your nose for the most part to avoid the thirty-person floundering-caused turbulent waters from flooding your throat. Grunt and heavy air expulsion as you tried to pull yourself out of the pool. Breathing at the speed of your push-ups and sit-ups, not necessarily the speed you needed or wanted...

Lower oxygen levels in your blood, mixed with constant blood flow adjustments between your brain and body made for a messed-up head.

After about five or six laps, I started to lose balance slightly when I stood up to get back in line. I widened my forward steps, something I had wanted to do to keep my pants from falling earlier, but this time to keep my whole body from falling.

After about eight or nine laps, my vision started to get blurry. And to top it off, when jumping back into the water each time, I was gradually sinking farther and farther down before coming up. I was in the deep end of the pool, so there was no floor to be found that could help me push back up. So, it took more and more energy to get moving down the pool with each lap.

Fatigue turned me into a brick in water.

When I was a brick, staying afloat took more energy. So, not only was I getting tired from the work, the work itself was getting more difficult as I got more tired.

With every move, I could feel my heart rate climbing, my chest pounding as the red thing barely larger than my fist tried to oxygenate my starving muscles and brain. But due to the breathing struggles, oxygen was in short supply.

Normally, I could control my heart rate by setting a pace for my breathing and movements. When the rest of my body was in a rhythm, my heart seemed to follow.

When I was running or swimming long distances, I could sing the Mickey Mouse song in my head. The tempo was nearly perfect to keep my legs, breathing, and heart rate in line.

"M...IC...K...EY...M...OU...SE...Mick..eyMouse ...*dum*...*dum*...Mick...eyMouse..." Over and over I would sing that damn song in my head. For long-distance exercises, it could be half an hour of that on repeat.

Now you understand why I was a little crazy. It might have been self-inflicted from a form of music torture. But it worked for me. I could stay paced and breathing.

However, it didn't work when you were constantly changing the pace or the activity. This exercise had the rhythm of a drummer with palsy. Swim and eggbeater in-and-outs were my endurance strategy's Kryptonite. Without being able to pace my breathing and heart rate, I was getting dizzy faster than I should have. And along with that came nausea....

Don't throw up, Tyler, I told myself silently.

If I have to throw up, I can't be the first one to do it.

I could feel it coming. My mouth was getting filled with saliva. I kept burping lightly to reduce the pressure on my throat. Which, in turn, made breathing even harder.

Don't be first. Don't be first.

Having lost count of how many laps we'd done, I think it was around ten or something, Coach had his first victim.

One of the guys who he'd had put the tarp on the other pool got to the edge of the pool and was about to pull himself out to do his sit-ups. He put his hands on the deck and made an attempt to get out. He got halfway up when he dropped back down, face at pool drain level, and let it rip.

Oh, another part of that "other contaminant" group in the pool filter manuals was vomit. It was pretty common for swimmers and water polo players to throw up at practice. Glorious, isn't it?

Coach, now standing on the deck over the kid who puked, put the whistle to his lips and blew about five or six fast tweets signaling the end of the exercise.

"And this is why warm-ups are so important, Nick. Your body is cussing you out for getting lazy and not listening to my instructions."

That might have not been entirely physiologically accurate, but his underlying message was still valid.

Turning to face the rest of the pool, he said loudly. "Everyone take a minute to catch your breath and drink a little bit of water. Next we will do a bit of passing before breaking out into groups to run some offensive and defensive drills."

Grabbing my water bottle from the deck behind me, I took a small sip. Mainly, I needed to push my encroaching saliva back to where it belonged. Little steps to keep from throwing up. I knew if I took too large of a drink from the bottle, it would probably come back to visit.

Spencer walked up to me and asked jokingly, "Still alive?"

That was the second time today people were surprised I wasn't dead yet. Did I look that pathetic? I knew it was a pretty common thing to say after some exercise or a crappy day, but I didn't see anyone else getting asked today. Why was it always me?

"Yeah. I shot up a ton of steroids and snorted some cocaine before practice. It gave me the energy and strength I needed," I joked back.

"Good. We have a pro-drug policy here. Anything you need to get the job done works for us. Just be sure to share when you get some."

I let off a small smile, too tired to laugh. "Sounds good. I'll hook you up with my guy when I am conscious enough to remember his name. Right now, I barely know where I am."

"When Coach gets in the mood to teach a lesson like that, we call the pool Poseidon's Butthole," he said.

"What's it called when he's in a good mood?" I asked.

"Poseidon's Kiss," he responded quickly, not having to think too hard. It clearly wasn't made up on the spot. Must've been real.

"That sounds pretty harmless."

With a chuckle, Spencer responded, "You know when you are taking a shit in a porta-potty at some county fair and your turd causes a splash so big that the blue, inky water filled with everyone else's shit and piss splashes up and hits your ass? That's Poseidon's Kiss. Good mood or bad, you're getting fucked. Just expect to get fucked the first half of every practice, and you will never be surprised."

"After class today, I wasn't expecting Coach to be so evil. Mr. Hunter in the classroom and Coach on the deck are insanely different people," I said.

"Just wait, I hear he grades his students like he plans workouts," Spencer warned with a more serious tone.

"Great..."

"Oh, come on. It won't all be bad. If you survive drills today, you might get to push your body to the brink of collapse every day with us. Aren't you excited about that?"

"Only if I can keep my suit on the whole time," I half joked.

"Yeah... Please try to keep it on. We have a hard enough time convincing people this sport isn't gay."

"Well, with names like Poseidon's Kiss, and Poseidon's Butthole, you aren't exactly helping your case there," I said with a smile, feeling better now that my brain was getting oxygen again.

"Ha! Fair enough."

The rest of practice went as expected. Coach led us all through some standard six-versus-six drills, along with some man-up/man-down drills simulating how to take advantage of or defend against when a player got ejected from a foul.

Whenever I played with a new team, it took some time to adjust to shooting styles. In the first part of practice, I let a few too many shots get past me. Brandon, the cocky skin-and-bones kid from my earlier exposure situation, was smiling with every goal he made on me.

I was starting to worry about my position on the team. I needed to hold my own. Brandon was on the JV team. If I couldn't block his shots, I'd be put on the freshman team. On top of that, I'd only made one friend today, Spencer, and he was on JV as well. So, I had extra motivation to make JV just to stick around him and avoid being a loner again.

Seeing me struggle to block some shots, Coach didn't seem too concerned.

"Tyler, you have excellent form and you seem to be able to read the shooters really well, but your reaction time seems to be killing your delivery. You're getting to where you need to be, but fractions of a second too late."

As I worried he'd be disappointed and tell me to get out and dry off, he continued, "The angle work you're doing is something I've been trying to get the other goalies to learn for weeks. I'll make you a deal. We'll teach you how I got their reaction times down if you help me teach them how to cut down the shooter's angles? After that, I think we will all be in a solid defensive position. Deal?"

Shocked at how well that turned out, I smiled and nodded my head. "Works for me, Coach."

Looking back at the team, Coach said jokingly, "If we can get your reaction time down, God help all these other bastards trying to score on you.

"All right, guys, Nick is getting all pruned from the bath. It's time to shut down for the day. I want every ball put in the cart, every goal pulled out, and all the tarps rolled out before anyone gets dressed. Nice work, everyone."

He blew his whistle a few times for good measure. I don't know why; we'd all heard him say we were done. Maybe it was just a coach thing.

He started to walk toward his office, located on the far side of the pool deck near the rooms with the filtration systems.

Had I made the team? He didn't pull everyone in like he had for Luke. Was he prepping to tell me privately I didn't make it? Damnit. Why had he said that shit about helping my reaction times if he knew I wouldn't make it?

What a dick.

Just as I was working myself up with anger and disappointment, he turned back and said loudly, "Oh, yeah. Hey, everyone, say hi to your new JV goalie, Tyler. Sorry, Chris, you're not the only guy that we will be pelting polo balls at this year."

A grin started to show on Coach's face as he looked down at me in the pool. He'd known I would bug out, and he was just messing with me.

Sadistic.

I liked him.

Spencer swam up behind me, and putting both hands on my shoulders, he shoved me under water—the subtle water polo equivalent of the baseball team putting the guy who hit the winning home run on their shoulders after rounding the bases.

Like a version of a punch to the shoulder that allowed the dunker to look cool as he put the dunkee in a position where he struggled to breathe. Win-win.

After I surfaced, Spencer and a few other guys were laughing and nodded in my direction. Except Brandon, but I didn't care.

No one tells you that daydreaming in class, flashing your dick at strangers, almost vomiting in a pool, and allowing the other team to score repeatedly on you would work out for you in the end.

But it seemed to for me.

Today, at least.

I got dressed under my towel, this time much more carefully than before. I didn't want to risk getting arrested for indecent public exposure on my first day... again.

Spencer was dressed now, with his suit and goggles taking their place on his shoulder, held there with his towel. He didn't seem to care about his shirt getting wet. That would bug the hell out of me.

He was in a huddle with Brandon and a few other guys from the team off by the entrance to the pool. They looked pretty serious and kept looking over in my direction. Was there something wrong? Did they not agree with Coach's decision to put me on the team?

I should have done better at blocking those shots. Damnit, it had taken too long to adjust to their shooting style.

I'd like to see you guys have faster reactions to new shooters after doing all those in-and-outs.

Whatever.

Spencer, after nodding his head at the guys as they left the pool deck, walked over to where I was getting dressed.

"Hold on to that towel tightly, Tyler. I don't want to see your dick twice in one day," he joked.

"Funny, I was just about to drop the towel on purpose. You guys seemed to have liked it."

Smiling, Spencer said casually, "Not sure about you, but most guys here prefer to see only one dick the rest of their lives—their own. We had to reset the 'days since last dick incident' calendar today. Not ideal."

"What are they going to do about gym locker rooms... or porn? There are dicks everywhere. Sounds like insecure denial if you ask me," I said, pretending like it was no big deal to me what had happened.

"Ha! Maybe." He laughed. "But if I had their dicks instead of mine, I'd be insecure and in denial too."

I cracked a small smile and let out a quick burst of air from my nose as a laugh escaped.

"Hey, look, Brandon is having the starters on the team over to his place for a small party on Friday night. It took a bit of convincing, mainly due to his dick insecurity, but you're invited. You'll get a kick out of his house. It's insane."

"Yeah, okay," I said, a little pensively. "But only if I can use the opportunity to embarrass myself in new ways. It's kind of an Olympic sport for me."

"I noticed," he said as he shook his head side to side with a smile. "See you tomorrow in class," he said, making the same nod he had to the other guys before walking away.

"See you later," I responded.

"Wait!" I said louder than I intended to. "What's your last name? I can't find you on my app."

"McLaughlin," he said back with a casual smile. "But if you follow me, you are going to see some weird shit. Be prepared."

4

As I finished up deck changing, successfully this time, Luke signaled to me from the bleachers that he was ready to go home. The rest of varsity was long gone, but he'd stuck around to give me a ride home.

He drove this crappy hand-me-down car that had a busted transmission that shifted whenever it felt like it. It also had full-length ribbon-esque stickers on its sides like from those cheap paper cups in dental offices, and an old-school interior style. I don't mean like a real leather Camaro or Mustang old-school style. I mean like a carpet-lined shoebox that has wheels from the days before they learned how to bend metal sheets, complete with a lawnmower engine and upholstery made of sandpaper. You know, from when cars were made by riveting together metal panels from third-world country slum shacks.

I'm exaggerating, but you get the idea.

It used to be our dad's old car from after college. He drove it a million and seven miles before upgrading to his new SUV. When Luke got his driver's license, my dad wanted him to drive something "with character" first.

In our old town in Southern California, it fit right in. It was a town outside of all the tourist stops and businesses.

Most people couldn't afford to live in those places, so they lived in towns like ours and commuted in.

I'm sure at his old school Luke had fit in perfectly with his car, parking right alongside a tractor and golf cart. Joking, but not entirely…

However, this school would be different.

This high school was smack in the middle of a big tech area of Northern California, just outside of the famous Silicon Valley. The kids at this school were the sons and daughters of some pretty disturbingly wealthy parents. Remember that guy who donated the multimillion-dollar pool just so his son could play? Yeah.

So, the cars the students drove were appropriate to that world of elevated social status.

When we'd gotten to school this morning, Luke parked between two cars that were nicer than anything my family had ever owned. At first, I'd thought we were accidentally in the teachers' parking lot, but all the student parking passes hanging from the rearview mirrors said we were in the right place.

Normally, the teacher and staff parking had nicer cars than the student lot did, mainly because teachers made more money than students did working in fast-food drive-through windows.

But not here.

At this school, students' parents made so much money that they could throw more toward their kids' casual needs than teachers could spend on necessities.

This was just one more thing that would keep me from fitting in here.

Our parents weren't rich.

Luke and I weren't going to get a sports car for graduation, a vacation to Spain for a summer trip, or a job at our parents' law firm filing papers for triple the hourly wage a normal admin would make to get "work experience."

We got what we got. We made what we made. That was it.

It wasn't that my parents didn't love us enough to give us the best. They loved us enough to give us what they could.

Our dad worked in IT. Back in Southern California, he worked from home since most of IT had to do with accessing computers and servers remotely. He would wake up in the morning, take us to school, and head back home to sit in his office until we had to be picked up at the end of the day.

It worked for him. He was a quiet guy who liked to work on his own, at his own pace. As you've seen by now from my introverted social skills, there should be no doubt that I hailed from this guy genetically.

Our mom ran a daycare center at a huge biotech company in the main city down there. They had so many employees that they had their own daycare center on-site. She would leave for work a few hours before we got up for school so she could be there to greet the kids as their parents showed up for work early in the morning.

Since the parents at that company worked a normal eight-to-five job, my mom often didn't get home until after seven or eight p.m. She was there from the time the first kid showed up at sunrise, and didn't leave until the last one went home around sunset.

Last month, my dad got a promotion, and the company told him he needed to move up to Northern California to work out of their headquarters. He wasn't remotely logging into systems and fixing things anymore; he needed to be in the office to train and manage a small team of new techs working on the main data center servers.

About three weeks ago, we all packed up into two cars after the moving truck drove off ahead of us and made the trip north.

"So, are you going to sell this thing and get a Ferrari? It doesn't exactly match the decor around here," I asked Luke.

"Hell no. Why would I want a sterile thing that needs to be waxed every weekend?" he said with a chuckle.

"It doesn't bother you having a piece of shit in a pile of gold bricks?" I asked.

"Why would it? Also, dude, enough with the metaphors and analogies. We talked about this. It's annoying as fuck. Speak like a normal person."

"It's just how my head works when I'm tired, okay? Deal with it," I said seriously before answering his question, "I don't know. All the other cars are so much cooler."

"Why should I care if they think my car is cool or not? They didn't do anything special to earn their fancy cars, so it doesn't really say much about them as a person. It says more about their parents than it does them.

"If they are so fixated on determining my coolness based on my car," he continued, "then they probably aren't someone whose opinion I care about. No way in hell do I want a crazy car payment just to have something shiny that will make shallow people like me."

It made a lot of sense logically. But logic didn't work in high school. I'd never been able to not care. I wouldn't have the best thing or be the coolest, but I seemed to try hard to not give them ammunition to think otherwise.

Luke never seemed to care. He always fit in wherever he was, so I don't think he could see it from where I sat.

The logic seemed to work out just fine for him.

I must have been sitting there silently for too long, because he jumped back in.

"Look. Who gives a shit what people think about this car? Who gives a shit if they care that our parents aren't millionaires? Who gives a shit if they saw your dick?"

He'd seen that? Fuck...

He laughed and continued, "I get it. New schools suck and asshole rich kids make them worse. But people will like you and think you're cool, and people will think you're a poor dork with a tiny dick. It's unavoidable, no matter what you

44

do. Just hang out with the people who you like and like you back... and stop showing your dick to the judgmental people."

"Ha-ha, okay," I said, but I wasn't fully on board.

It wasn't that easy for me to brush off what people thought. Sometimes, it bothered me so much that I would have fictitious arguments with them in my head. Not when they were in front of me. But if they said something in passing, I'd think about it too much and counter them silently with some well-organized speech hours later in my head.

I'd never be able to come up with those kinds of speeches on the fly. They were honed and perfected after dozens of walk-throughs in my head. Sometimes, I'd just stand in a shower perfecting some monologue that would never be spoken out loud before realizing I'd been doing it for so long that the water started to turn cold and it snapped me back to reality.

Just ignore them? Yeah, it wasn't that easy.

"They use a lot of chlorine in this pool. You stink."

"I didn't have time to shower after my practice like you did, remember?"

"Whatever, you still stink. It's burning my nose," he said with a grin as he rolled down his driver-side window with the crank by his left knee. No electric windows here.

The conversation must have been bothering me because the fresh air that started flying around me made me feel better. Or maybe it was the chlorine.

Now that the wind was carrying away my odor, he reached down to his phone and turned on some music. He wasn't upset that there was no Bluetooth in his car and he needed to plug in an aux cable that he pulled through a crack in the dashboard. He was just happy he could have his music in the car.

A few seconds later, a loud electric guitar hit, complete with bass drum, snare, and cymbal smashing through the speakers, followed by brief silence. It only took that one hit for me to know what it was.

He loved Metallica.

His favorite song was "Master of Puppets," and it started blaring through his speakers.

For someone who had his shit together, didn't do drugs, and had a stable view of life and where he fit into it, he really seemed to like music about hardcore drug use and the world falling apart.

"How do you listen to this shit all the time? It just sounds like chaos to me. Stresses me out," I said, annoyed this was on the stereo again for the thousandth time.

"Order all the time is boring. Sometimes you need a bit of chaos to shake things around and remind you to wake up."

"Deep," I said with an eye roll.

He ignored me and turned the volume up a bit higher, the bass now making the cheap speakers in the car doors distort, whining to Luke that he was toeing the line between them blasting music and blowing out, silent forever.

5

Houses were crazy expensive in the Bay Area. Even after my dad's decent raise for his new gig, he could barely afford a small three-bedroom townhouse. Every building in this town felt like someone put it in a vise and squeezed the ever-living shit out of it until it resembled a Dr. Seuss building the width of two Whoville citizens.

We didn't complain because we still had our own rooms, but I already missed having a real backyard and normal-sized bedrooms. Apparently concrete slabs with grass growing out of the cracks from California earthquakes qualified as a yard here.

After my mom got a new job, maybe we would be able to move to somewhere with more wiggle room and with more than six blades of grass. But we were stuck here for the time being.

After casually executing a perfect curbside parallel park, Luke turned off the car's ignition and the music died, leaving us in momentary silence. Luke rolled up the window with a few aggressive cranks of the handle and stepped out of the car.

My whole body was exhausted. When the car vibration stopped and the music went silent, I just sat there in the seat. I didn't want to move. The idea of lifting my arm, opening the door, stepping out, and walking sounded nearly impossible.

Luke was now standing at the front bumper and slapped the hood of the car with his hand a few times. It startled me a little bit and I looked up.

"Are you coming?" he asked, looking slightly concerned.

I grabbed my backpack and polo bag off the floor in front of me, opened the door, and stepped out.

"I mean, those in-and-outs looked painful, but you're a zombie. You okay?"

"Yeah, I'm just tired," I said. It wasn't just physical fatigue; I was tired of thinking. Tired of talking. I don't know why it hit me so hard, so fast. But as soon as the chaos blaring out of his car stereo abruptly stopped, I felt like every part of my body was ten pounds heavier. I just didn't feel like I wanted to move.

The fatigue was really starting to set in. My legs were somewhat numb, almost like they were asleep, but without the pins and needles keeping you from moving them around. They moved fine, just sluggish, and they didn't feel connected to my body anymore.

Walking along the earthquake-and-tree-root-cracked concrete pathway to the front door, I felt like the whole world was just…quieter than it had been before. Maybe it was the lack of Metallica blasting, but I could feel my focus narrowing like it had during the earlier workout. Standing up from the car must have messed with my blood flow like the in-and-outs had.

This was going to be a long season.

As we walked through the front door to our new home, a familiar scent welcomed us in. I knew exactly what it was as soon as it hit my nostrils, and instantly, a great feeling of relief hit my whole body. My starving stomach stopped growling, as if to say, *I'll be nice if you let me have some of that...* My head, still a little dazed from fatigue both from practice and the normal drama of the day, was pulled awake.

We were having ribs for dinner.

My mom made these ribs that were half-baked, half-barbecued, and soaked in barbecue sauce. They were so juicy, and they fell off the bone. Grabbing the edge of the bone and using a few fingers from my free hand to hold the slab down, I could casually lift the bone free of the meat. The extracted bone, now completely free, left every piece of meat it used to be attached to on the plate in one piece. If I did this half a dozen times, I'd have an inch-thick juicy slab of boneless rib meat ready to be destroyed.

Since my mom was still looking for work up here, she was home most of the day. As a result, she decided to cook more. My grandmother was a chef back in the day and teased my mom all the time about us eating out or eating my dad's college-dorm-quality food. Giving in to her peer pressure, my mom kept saying she wanted to pull her old recipes out and give a few a shot.

This ribs recipe was one of the few she'd pulled out a few years ago, and it instantly became all of our favorites to the point where we could have probably afforded a mansion and sports cars for Luke and me if we didn't have such a huge chunk of our budget allocated to meat.

After a practice like that, I didn't want a mansion or a car with leather seats. I just wanted some meat and a nap. So far, I knew I'd get the first part. The second seemed like a pipe dream.

The entry to the house was a tiny hallway that opened up into a small office den off to the right, currently used to house all our unpacked moving boxes.

To the left was a narrow staircase that did a quick turn up before dumping out in another small hallway with my parents' room off the right and Luke's and my rooms to the left, mine at the end.

At the end of the entry hallway, the living room opened up the space and had large floor-to-ceiling windows. I'm sure the architect was thinking this would make the room feel even bigger than it was, but they opened the view up to show the depressingly small backyard and fence blocking the view of our neighbors' even smaller one.

The living room had a bar-style counter off to the right, separating it from the kitchen, which opened to a dining room, bringing the kitchen and dining room to match the living room in size.

Luke went straight upstairs to drop his things, but I was too tired to think about stairs. I dropped my bags on the floor as I entered the living room and made my way to the kitchen, the smell of the ribs pulling me in.

As I rounded the half wall into the kitchen, my mom greeted me with, "Hi, honey, how was school?" She was head down in the refrigerator, buried deep, looking for a second bottle of BBQ sauce.

She turned around and looked into my eyes with a kind smile. After a quick pause, and before I could respond, her face turned a little investigative. "Wow, that bad, huh?"

"What's that supposed to mean?" I asked defensively.

"Well, you look really...tired? I don't know. What's wrong? What happened?" she asked with a concerned tone in her voice.

"It was fine. I'm fine. Just tired," I said, not wanting to get into the details. I just wanted to get some food, take a long shower to wash off the chlorine, and hide in my room to recover from the day. The last thing I wanted to do was relive all the awkwardness and drama. I knew she was just asking because she cared, but I didn't want to talk about it.

"Well...okay," she said, clearly not believing me but not pressing the subject.

"He had a *great* day." Luke must have heard my answer from around the corner and felt the need to jump into the conversation. "Did he tell you he flashed his dick to the whole pool deck?" Luke jokingly threw out there like it was some great accomplishment.

"What?" our mom asked with eyes wide, first at Luke, then turning her gaze to me. "How? Why? What?"

"It wasn't like that. My towel fell while I was deck changing... Luke, you ass."

"Don't call him an ass. In Luke's defense, it sounds funny," she said, clearly trying not to laugh herself. I didn't feel like she was trying to join the group in making fun of me. It felt more like she was trying to make it lighter than it was to reduce its impact on me.

"After that display, you must have made the team on the spot," she continued.

"He did. But as expected, his tiny wiener wasn't enough. He had to earn it. They beat up JV hard. He hung in pretty well," Luke added as he walked toward the snack cupboard.

"Luke, don't eat anything. I'm clearly making a big meal. Just wait. It will be done in thirty minutes. Go clear off the boxes and set the table," she said with a stern tone to her voice.

As she looked back to me, her tone switched back to the caring one she had earlier. "That's great! I'm so proud of you. I'd be prouder if you kept it in your pants, but you're getting closer to the age where I knew that would be a challenge. So I should have seen this coming."

"Funny," I said, bouncing eye contact between the two of them so they could see the frustrated expression on my face.

Just as Luke was about finished setting the table, Dad walked through the front door. With his messenger bag slung over his shoulder, he dropped his keys in the bowl by the door and made his way into the kitchen, where we all were.

He looked beat. He looked even more tired than I was. What was the IT version of in-and-outs? Whatever it was, he must have done it.

"Hey, guys" he said casually to Luke and me as he walked over to Mom. Giving her a light kiss, he said "Hi, honey."

"How was your day?" she asked. After his "Hi, honey," this felt like some canned TV family conversation starter.

"Exhausting. We had four new system admins start today, so I sent them to the fighting pits under the data center to decide which three would get to stay past the probation period. I definitely worked up a sweat just trying to clean up the mess," he said with a deadpan expression on his face.

"Why didn't you make the other three clean up the mess for you?" Luke asked casually.

"I don't know, it just seemed a little cruel. I didn't want to seem too hard on them their first day."

Sarcasm was a genetic trait passed down through all Lawson offspring. My grandfather, my dad, Luke, and I? Fluent.

"Great, thanks, Robert. Let's teach them that lying and sarcasm are good. I have a hard enough time getting them to take things seriously," Mom responded with an *I'm tired of this shit* look on her face.

Not only had she dealt with Dad's sarcasm and bad jokes for about a quarter century, the idea of adding additional players to the game must have seemed too exhausting for her to sit back and let happen.

"Ribs? Nice. I'm going to drop my bag and wash up. I'll be back in a sec," he said, clearly refusing to respond to Mom's poke.

I think frustrating her with his humor was part of the fun for him. Like the eye rolls resulting from his dad jokes were the whole reason to make them. Not for the laugh but for the frustration.

He was a funny guy, but in a different way. With most humor, the comedian seemed to get most of their satisfaction from the laughter and positive reactions to their jokes. But his humor was more about poking for other reactions. Not a laugh but some other reaction. Like it was more for him than anyone else. I heard that a lot of comedians were funny because of super-low self-esteem, and they just wanted the room to like them. So, they said jokes that make people feel good. If you felt good, you liked the person who made you feel that way.

Not Dad. I don't know, but I'd never felt like he cared if you liked him more after his jokes. You could almost never ask him a question and expect a serious response. He'd often answer your question, but in a roundabout way that mixed wit, sarcasm, and deviousness.

It definitely made my mom's dinner parties interesting. Mom would host some friends for dinner where she would expertly navigate and lead the conversation. Then, Dad would chime in almost out of nowhere with a sarcastic joke and the rest of the table would, with a cartoonish eye roll like Mom just did, broadcast an *oh, Robert* expression on their faces. Not in a negative way, but with a smile and a shrug.

Sometimes, he would say something just to push the comfort level in the room and fish for reactions. Those were my favorite. Something just outside appropriate dinner party behavior, but not bad enough to warrant sleeping on the couch. Boring dinner parties were now unpredictable. It made you curious where things would go next.

For someone so clean-cut in appearance and demeanor (usually), he sure enjoyed instigating a little chaos, if only just to observe the aftermath. Maybe this was like what Luke had been talking about in the car. Shake things up to keep it interesting. Like father, like son.

Sometimes, I thought my mom liked it. But I didn't think she would ever admit it.

As we all sat down to the table, Mom brought out a giant metal serving plate covered in ribs. It was glorious. Time slowed down, doves flew around behind her, orchestra music started playing… Okay, not quite, but it felt like it could happen.

53

After dropping it in the center of the small table for us all to grab a share, she took her seat at the end opposite Dad.

With my brain now on autopilot, I reached out and grabbed a massive slab off the tray and plopped it on my plate. *Need. Food.*

"Well so much for ladies first," Dad said with a judgmental stare in my direction.

"Sorry," I said, quickly glancing in Mom's direction, but eyes down at the table in front of her, avoiding eye contact.

As the rest of the table grabbed their share, Mom burst up from her chair, exclaiming, "I almost forgot," and rushed back into the kitchen.

She returned a few seconds later with two big pots. Starting with Dad, she scooped up a ladle full of mashed potatoes and dropped it on each plate. On the second pass, she swapped pots and dropped a pile of green beans on the plates, right next to the potatoes.

Damnit, I hated green beans.

Before she could make it around to me, I quickly moved the meat and potatoes around the plate so there wasn't enough space left for the green beans.

"Nice try," she said with a grin as she scooped up a pile larger than she'd given anyone else as punishment and plopped it right on top of everything else, leaving it up to me to sort, before walking back to her chair and serving herself.

"So? How was day one?" Dad asked, glancing back and forth between Luke and me, waiting for a response.

"Any issues joining the team or with classes?" he added, still fishing for responses. We didn't avoid the questions deliberately. We were just face deep in the food, barely leaving enough time to breathe, let alone talk.

"All... good," Luke said, forcing a swallow.

"Thanks for the details, Luke. Tyler, anything of substance to add to that quality description of events?" Dad shifted his gaze toward me this time.

"Sure…um… It was okay. The water polo coach, Mr. Hunter, is actually my physics teacher. Wasn't expecting that. But he seems cool. He's a brutal coach, but I think physics will be cool."

"What do you mean by brutal?" he asked, seemingly not out of concern—he knew how hard the sport was already—but out of curiosity.

"He just doesn't seem to take much crap, and his workouts are intense," I said, trying to sum up that whole experience with one sentence.

"Well, since I'm not allowed to beat you guys up at home after that domestic violence incident, might as well let a stranger do it for me," Dad joked.

"Ha-ha," Mom said loudly and forcefully at my father with a judgmental look on her face.

He looked back with a light smile, like a little kid who farted did waiting for the room to realize what had just gone down. After a few seconds, a little smile appeared on her face.

"So! I was thinking…" Dad abruptly said, ending the silence. "Now that we are getting settled and we have a fenced-in yard, how about we get a dog?"

"What?" Mom asked, shocked, clearly not in the decision process for this before he'd brought it to the table. "No. You go to work; the boys go to school. I will have to take care of it and do all the work."

I was instantly excited. We had a dog named Garfunkel when I was little, but I don't remember much. He passed away when I was five from cancer. I think it hit my Dad pretty hard. He had him for about twelve years before he died, and he hadn't seemed to want a new one the rest of my childhood. I'd asked…well, sort of begged… a lot over the past few years, but there were a lot of excuses why we couldn't get one.

"Don't worry, you'll have a food vacuuming shadow around the house during the day, and Tyler can take responsibility for it the rest of the time," Dad said, making me almost jump out of my chair.

I looked back and forth between them fast, waiting to hear what magical words came out of their mouths next.

"Nah, Tyler doesn't want to do it," Dad said calmly before looking down at his plate and bringing a fork full of mashed potatoes up to his mouth.

"*What*? Yes, I do!" I almost barked at him, completely missing the sarcasm in his comment.

"Well, you are excited for your physics class. You might need all the friends you can get. We might have to buy one for you in case they don't want to come naturally," Luke teased.

"He's got a point," Dad joined in, looking to Mom for a response.

"Tyler? Is this something you can handle? I'm not cleaning up its shit. I cleaned up after Gar, I've changed Luke's diapers, I've changed yours, I've changed them at work for years, and chances are I'll have to change your father's someday… I'm not cleaning up after it. That's enough dealing with excrement for one lifetime."

"I can do it!" I said loudly, unable to hold in my enthusiasm.

After a few agonizing seconds, complete with uncomfortable stares between Mom and Dad… "Okay, fine," she said, sounding defeated. "Don't make me regret this, guys."

The rest of dinner was a blur. Everyone ate, chatted, ate some more… But I wasn't paying attention anymore. My mind was spinning about the dog. What breed would I get? Did I want a male or female? What would its name be?

Today was insane. The stress of school, making the team, the physical fatigue… It didn't matter. I was getting a dog.

The rest of the week went by without any major issues. The first day of school fell on a Wednesday. I felt like they knew how crazy the first days were, so they limited the exposure.

Like radiation.

They knew bare skin exposed to the sun would kill you eventually from cancer, but they were cool with telling you to go frolic in the desert without sunscreen. But don't worry, they wouldn't make you hug a solid rod of uranium.

So, three days was manageable. For the most part...

As practice came to an end, I deck changed successfully now that I was getting the hang of it. After throwing my wet towel with my suit rolled up inside of it into my polo bag, I grabbed my backpack and started walking toward where Luke parked his car to ride home.

Tonight was the JV party at Brandon's house, so I needed to run home to shower and change. Brandon still didn't seem to like me, so this was going to be uncomfortable.

We still hadn't spoken to each other one-on-one. We'd been in the same area together and practiced together, but we hadn't been social. Maybe that would change tonight, but I doubted it.

As I was stepping off the pool deck, Spencer came around the corner.

"Yo! Tyler," he said to get my attention.

"What's up?"

"You coming to Brandon's tonight? Should be interesting," he said with a grin on his face. "Maybe you two will find out you love each other, get matching rainbow swimsuits, and get married."

"Yes to coming to the party, and *what the fuck?* to the rest of what you just said."

"Okay, okay, he's not your type." He laughed. "We were going to grab some drinks in a few minutes, so you have twenty dollars to pitch in? Or do you have some you could bring?"

I had never been to a high school party or bought alcohol, for that matter. I don't know why, but I was suddenly nervous for some reason. Mom and Dad weren't so crazy strict that the thought of alcohol would get me in trouble with them. They seemed pretty realistic about it all. Seeing Luke the last years, they'd let him sneak a beer every once in a while. Moderation instead of abstinence seemed to be their standard lesson.

When Luke had come home pretty wasted one night after hanging out with friends last year, they hadn't given him too much shit. Just made him ride his hangover as he did his normal weekend chores. I think mowing the lawn on a hundred-degree Southern California summer day with a raging hangover was enough for him to understand what he'd done wrong.

"I've only got ten dollars on me. Is that okay? I can pay you back later, but I don't have any booze," I responded, reaching into my pocket and pulling out some cash.

"Yeah, that's cool. I'll cover you," he said, taking the cash from my hand and putting it into his pocket.

"Thanks. I won't drink much, so don't think I'm going to be mooching off you," I said, trying to subtly hint at my not really wanting to drink.

"Ha," he laughed. "You're the new guy. You won't have much of a choice. You're getting shitfaced."

What did I say? *I don't really drink? I haven't drunk like that before?* No, I couldn't let him see how much of a loser I was...

I must have just stood there silently for too long trying to figure out what to say next, because Spencer jumped in. "Don't worry, it will be fun."

"Okay, sounds good," I said casually, trying not to show what I was really thinking.

As Spencer left, I made my way over to Luke's car, where he was already reclining in the driver seat, blasting some music with the windows down. As I approached, he kicked on the engine and raised his seat back up for the drive home.

Stepping into the passenger side, I threw my bags at my feet and put on my seat belt. Luke, now pulling out onto the main road, leaving the high school parking lot, turned down the music a bit and looked over to me.

"So, are you going to the freshman party?" he asked, teasing, knowing it wasn't the freshman team.

"It's JV, but yeah, I think I'll go. Do you think you would be able to pick me up when it's done?" I asked.

"What? You don't want Mom and Dad to come pick you up?" he said with a laugh and grin back in my direction. "I think so. When will you be done? I'll be going over to Brad's house, but I'll probably be done when you are."

Varsity must have been doing their own party tonight, because I thought Brad was one of their starters. The name was familiar.

I didn't know how Luke did it. He so calmly threw out that he was going to a party with some new people, and it sounded as casual as just going to a movie or something. Just the thought of this party was making me stress. I could still tell my heart rate was trying to recover from Spencer asking for money to buy alcohol.

"I don't know, maybe around eleven?" I said.

"Okay, just text me when you find out and I'll come over. I kind of want to see this house. If his parents could shovel out over a million dollars just to build this pool, their house must be insane."

Wait, that kid was Brandon? Suddenly this had gotten more complicated.

"It was Brandon's parents who did that?" I asked, surprised that Luke knew, and I didn't see how Brandon was on my team and not his.

"Yeah, his dad is some tech CEO or something. The rumor is he sold his last company for close to a billion dollars."

"Jesus..." I couldn't even imagine that. We were sitting in a car worth maybe two thousand dollars, and I was about to go to the house of someone on such a different level that the toilet could cost that much...

So, not only was I going to a stranger's house, but there would be alcohol, and it would be a crazy mansion where I'd be afraid to touch anything, knowing that if it broke, it would be my life's savings to replace it.

It was going to be even more opportunity for me to stand out from the crowd. Like I said before, I didn't come from money. Being around it was uncomfortable, especially if people knew that I didn't.

6

Luke gave me a ride to the party on his way to Brad's house. After about a fifteen-minute drive, we took a turn into a gated community on the outside of town.

My earlier fears were creeping up on me as soon as we made the turn into the driveway. For starters, you couldn't even see the house from the entrance to the driveway. It had two pillars on the sides with an open gate. Yes, a gated house within a gated community. Seemed excessive.

What's weird was it felt like we were approaching a nicer version of a Scooby Doo evil mansion. There was no lightning, dense fog, or werewolf howling in the background; this was California after all. But even in the presence of a sunset without a cloud in the sky, I felt like something was wrong. Not in a *there is a murderer in that house, and we are going to unmask them* sort of way. More like, *be on your toes.*

As uncomfortable as I'd been before, I was near supernova levels now—a star at a near-catastrophic level of instability.

The driveway had a gradual right bank up the side of a hill, covered in trees. As we got near the top of the hill, the trees turned into massive fields of perfectly manicured grass. Grass covered the entire top of the hill, with a huge mansion placed dead center of its highest point.

Three stories tall, four-car garage, huge double front doors, and a sculpted water fountain taller than I was in the middle of a gravel turnabout. After Luke drove around the fountain, he stopped just short of the stairs leading up to the front doors.

Hesitant to open the doors and get out, I put my hand on the door handle and just sat for a second. I knew I needed to get out of the car, but right now I was safe. It was just Luke and me in the car. As soon as I opened the door, it would be just me in a strange environment.

I still didn't have a lot of friends, only Spencer really. What if he wasn't here yet? Who would I talk to? What if I had to talk to strangers or the guys on the team who didn't like me? I didn't think the other players hated me; they didn't know me yet. But I didn't think they liked me yet either.

"So, are you going to get out? Or do I need to kick you out as I drive away, making you do a tuck and roll?" Luke jabbed at me.

"Yeah, just needed to think for a second."

"You looked like you were holding your breath. You okay?" he asked, concerned now.

"I'm fine. Just needed a second." I tried to play it cool, but I'm sure he could see my apprehension. "Thanks for the ride. I'll text you when I'm done."

I gave the handle a pull and, using my elbow, pushed open the car door. Stepping out didn't feel right. It felt like I was leaving the place I wanted to be behind, and it just felt… off.

After grabbing my hoodie sweatshirt off the seat, I closed the car door and waved Luke off. He pulled away, making the car engine rev up too high from the busted transmission. It took forever to shift from first to second gear, making it sound like he was trying to drag race. Since the car's engine was the size of a lawnmower, he just pulled away slowly. It really messed with a person's brain. They heard a car speeding off, but their eyes showed them a golf cart running out of batteries.

The noise from Luke's car must have been enough for people inside the house to hear. As I was making my way up the stairs to the front door, it surprisingly opened up. Caught off guard, I tripped and hit my shin on the edge of the top step.

A woman came through the door opening. She was a little older than my mom, but it was hard to tell through all the...upgrades... she'd made over the years. I didn't know how many parts were still original.

"Ouch! Are you okay?" she asked. "That looked like it hurt."

"Ye—yeah, I'm fine."

"Are you from Brandon's team? I'm his mother, Angela."

Struggling to look up and make eye contact, I reached out to shake her extended hand. "Yeah, I'm Tyler."

"Nice to meet you, Tyler. The boys are around the back by the pool. You can go around and meet them there if you want." She let go of my hand and pointed to her right. "Just follow that path and you'll see them. Do you want some ice for your leg first?"

"No, I'm okay, thanks," I said and turned to walk off. As I made my way back down the steps to the walkway, she seemed to stand there for a second and watch me walk away before going back inside. Maybe to make sure I didn't fall on my way down too...

Yes, that was an awkward introduction. Yes, I could have done better. But, no, I didn't know how. I mean, I understood how you were supposed to charismatically and casually introduce yourself and start a conversation with new people without sustaining injury or embarrassment. However, I didn't know how to make myself do it.

The only way I could describe it was it was like you spent your whole life practicing the guitar. You knew that a concert was coming up the next day, and you didn't want to screw it up. So, you practiced and practiced at home with some headphones hooked up to your amp until the chords and melody were solidified in your muscle memory. The next day, when you get on stage, you realize you forgot your guitar at home.

You're left standing there on stage in front of all those people empty handed, not knowing what to do next. After some awkward silence, and some mild mumbling from the audience like "is he okay?" someone rushes out to you from off stage and shoves a banjo into your hands, gives you a thumbs up, and runs off. So, now you have an instrument you don't really know how to play, but you know enough to try to strum at the strings. The "music" that comes out isn't what you practiced that would have made you sound like Santana. Instead, it's some terrible, off-key babble making you look like a toothless hillbilly.

You were prepared. You knew what to do. You thought you were ready.

Too bad.

You might argue that I didn't forget the guitar when meeting Brandon's mom, I just forgot how to play. But it wasn't like that. In my mind, I knew exactly how to play. But for some reason, I just couldn't get my body and voice to deliver what my brain was saying. Like some critical component was missing for the brain-to-reality connection to be made.

You knew the issue was one hundred percent your own. It was in your head. But you couldn't seem to avoid it. This made it even harder afterwards when you repeatedly relived the interaction in your mind.

Meeting new people was hard for me. Whenever I had to meet someone new, the first thought that jumped into my head was, *Why can't we just be past all the intros and be in the silent friend phase where you don't have to say anything to each other?* That way I wouldn't need to practice the guitar or remember to pack it in its case to bring with me to the concert. I could just show up and the concert would be done.

As I started to round the house along the path Brandon's mom had pointed me toward, the yard opened up to a crazy view of the Bay Area. The tree line on the hill was just far enough down the sides where the treetops were just out of the line of sight from the house. A million-dollar view was an understatement. Seeing how crazy expensive this town was, this had to be in the tens of millions.

I couldn't even imagine having enough money to look at a house like this and say, "Yeah, I can afford it. I'll take it."

The sun was just now passing below the horizon, leaving the Bay Area below speckled with home and streetlights. The gradual sloping of the hill in every direction you looked, illuminated softly by the landscape lighting, reminded me of those pictures from the International Space Station that showed the curvature of the green and blue earth below, with endless stars just beyond.

For a moment, I forgot where I was and just stood there. The view was slowly relaxing the anxiety I was feeling about the party.

I loved outer space.

In normal life I felt confined, surrounded, as if I was being held down to earth by its crushing gravity. The idea of floating with nothing around me, just floating in silence, seemed perfect. No awkward conversations with strangers. No deck changing mishaps. No tripping on stairs… just… nothing.

It sounded peaceful.

I used to think a lot about what it would be like to be an astronaut when I was little. When I found out they didn't send anyone up alone anymore like they did in the Mercury missions, and you were actually crammed into those tiny ships with a few other people, it instantly sounded terrible. Locked in something tiny for days, weeks, or months with the same people. No privacy, no escape. It seemed to ruin the attractiveness of visiting space.

My phone dinged in my pocket, signaling a new notification, snapping me back to reality. I pulled it out of my pocket to see that I was tagged in someone's social post.

It was a picture of my back. Right now. Staring at the view, with the caption: *@TylerH2O has been staring like this for three minutes not realizing I'm standing behind him.*

"You're really weird. You know that, right?"

I turned around quickly to see Spencer standing there with his backpack over his shoulder and cell phone in hand. Unlike in class, his backpack was clearly filled with several heavy and large things.

"Dude, you were just standing there staring at nothing," he said with a little laugh.

"Yeah, sorry, I was just looking at the view. And yes, I know I'm weird. You seriously posted that shit?"

"Yeah, I told you I post strange shit. But good. At least you know you're weird. Acceptance is the first step to recovery. Works for Alcoholics Anonymous; it will probably work for you." He had a pretty good grin on his face now.

"This place is crazy," I told him. "I had no idea it was Brandon's family who donated the pool. They are disgustingly rich."

"Yeah, they are. And he knows they are, unfortunately. I've been trying to keep him grounded since fifth grade."

"Is it working?" I asked.

"Nope," he said quickly and seriously.

"Cool."

"Come on, let's go find them," he said, starting the walk along the path, passing me. We made another turn around one of the house extensions and came to a massive illuminated and steaming pool. The pool had a special light that cycled through a dozen colors, gradually shifting the color of the water as we walked toward it.

Next to the pool was a small pool house. The pool house looked like a stand-alone, glass-walled living room complete with open double glass doors. Apparently having money meant everything got two doors. One was just...pedestrian, apparently. There was a coffee table covered in magazines, surrounded by comfortable-looking couches, flat-screen TV, bar, and a table to the side. All the lights were on, and music was playing on the speakers hanging from the walls.

It looked like most of the team was already there, maybe about ten guys. As Spencer walked through the open double glass doors, Brandon stood up from the couch and almost yelled.

"Finally! We were getting bored and almost opened up my dad's stuff."

Spencer walked over to the table in the corner and put his backpack down onto it with a loud clanging sound as the bottles inside it came to rest. He reached in and pulled out five bottles, each a different type of hard liquor. Rum, whiskey, something clear, which I assumed was vodka, and a couple others I didn't recognize.

Brandon looked over to Chris, who was now standing by the bar on the far wall, messing with a deck of cards. Brandon started issuing orders to the guys. "Chris, grab that bag of cups behind the bar. Let's get this started. If anyone posts this shit online, just kill yourself because it will be less painful than when I do it."

All the guys started making their way over to the table with the alcohol, reminding me of those videos of cows all rushing and circling around a bale of hay the farmer just dropped.

Brandon gave Nick a little shove with a laugh as he approached the table.

"Dude, you are last. Last party you drank up half of our booze."

"Fuck you," Nick replied with a little smile on his face. He let out a light chuckle. "Yeah, that was a fun night."

I stood in the back of the group waiting to see what happened. I didn't want to go up and get something. I'd known there would be alcohol, obviously. But I hadn't expected this to be only about drinking as soon as I got there. Maybe I could pass on this round and get something later. Maybe I could hold a cup so they'd think I was drinking.

The rest of the guys poured their drinks and started spreading out again, leaving just Spencer at the table pouring his own.

"Tyler, what do you want?" he asked looking back to me.

"No, I'm good. Thanks," I said softly, not wanting the other guys to hear me over the music.

"Oh, come on. You paid for some of this, might as well drink some," he said. He grabbed his cup and held it up to my face, giving it a light wiggle. "Give in to peer pressure," he said in a jokingly hypnotic voice. "I'll pour it. What do you like?"

I didn't know the answer to that. I'd never had hard alcohol before. Only sipped a beer and a little bit of wine with my family. Shit, he was going to know…

"Um, what are you having?" I tried to say casually, like I was cool with anything.

"I'm a rum guy," he said, pouring some of the brown liquid into a clichéd red plastic cup before handing it to me.

"Thanks," I said, tipping it slightly and looking in, hoping he'd only poured a little bit.

He hadn't.

As the guys started drinking, they spread out. Some put their suits on and jumped into the pool or sat in the jacuzzi. A few others went over to the tennis court around the back of the pool house (yes, there was a tennis court too—this place was insane) and started hitting tennis balls back and forth, quickly abandoning the rules and turning into a battle to pelt the other person as hard as you could.

All of them got louder and wilder as the levels in the bottles Spencer had brought got lower. One of the seemingly major advantages of throwing parties here was that there were no neighbors to be seen. No one to hear us. No noise complaints meant no cops.

I hung out in the pool house, trying to stay out of the bulk of the group. I hoped they wouldn't see that I was still holding the same drink Spencer had poured three hours before. Music played, guys drank, and time passed. The good thing was no one tried to talk to me too much or get me to do things. I was hoping this would continue until it was time to go home.

Spencer, Chris, Brandon, and Nick all came into the pool house laughing hard. Well, Nick wasn't laughing; he was holding a hand to his eye.

"Dude, Chris fucking nailed you with that ball," Brandon said, laughing harder now. "Go get some ice from the bar."

Nick gave them all a middle finger with his free hand before walking over to the bar.

I was sitting on the far side of the longer couches that surrounded the coffee table in the middle of the room. Spencer, Brandon, and Chris all grabbed seats in the spare spots and just sunk in. Like synchronized triplets, they spread out their bodies as if they'd just run a marathon and let out some deep breaths, audible over the music.

Spencer broke the silence between them.

"Okay, exercise and booze doesn't work. I'm getting the spins," he said with a laugh. Nick walked back over to us with a plastic bag of ice pressed to his face and grabbed a seat next to me on the couch.

"Well, the vodka didn't seem to mess with Chris's aim," he said with a frustrated tone. "That fucking hurt. I can feel my brain pulsing."

"That's not from the ball; that's your brain dying from lack of usage," Spencer said, laughing.

"Well, even with a dying brain, he isn't as messed up as Jake is," Brandon said.

Jake was a sophomore on our team, but I didn't know him that well. He never really spoke to anyone else.

"What do you mean? He's just quiet," Spencer said.

Brandon leaned forward. "I found out he's crazy. Seeing a shrink and on a ton of meds." He looked at the guys, fishing for reactions to what he must have felt was crazy news.

"What kind of meds?" Chris asked. "Did he, like, go Rambo and had to be put on something to mellow him out? Because it seems to be working." He let out a little laugh.

"I don't know. Like, I think he tried cutting himself or something and was put on antidepressants. I haven't seen scars or anything, but it makes sense," Brandon added, looking at each of us for a reaction. I tried not to show that this conversation was making me uncomfortable.

"If he's depressed, why doesn't he just come to these parties and drink or something? It's like he doesn't want to be normal and have fun. Booze is cheaper than pills," Spencer said with a laugh. "But if he's crazy, maybe he shouldn't come. Can you imagine if, like, whiskey tweaked him because of the meds and he went insane here?"

"I don't want that shit at my house. I guess it's good he didn't come," Brandon said.

Laughing, Nick turned to me. "Tyler, you're pretty weird. I guess it's good you aren't on meds to take your crazy to the next level. You seem to be the opposite with drinks. You've barely changed since the party started. Is there anything in your cup?"

He reached over and grabbed the plastic cup out of my hand, looking inside. "What number is this? Three? Four?"

"Three," I lied.

I was still on number one. "I don't know, it must just affect me less than you guys."

Brandon, now laughing loudly, said, "Tyler, the heavyweight! Yeah, I'm calling bullshit on that. I think you're nursing the shit out of your first."

Fuck. Now what?

I didn't want to drink, and I didn't want them to realize I was new to this. It was like I was trying to steal second base in baseball, and the first baseman with the ball was just waiting for me to pick where I was going. Was I going to second so he could throw it over for an out? Or was I going to try to make it back to first? Either way, the odds of coming out successfully from this weren't looking good....

"Finish that right now and go pour a new one," he commanded, everyone now looking at me. This was exactly what I didn't want to happen. Hours of success had just come crashing down in the last minute.

"No, I'm good," I said, trying to back out of the order.

"Fuck that. Drink!" Brandon insisted.

I looked around the room at the other guys. They were all watching me now with smiles on their faces. Looking to Spencer, hoping he'd help me get out of this, I was greeted with the same damn smile the others had, his head bobbing up and down in agreement with the crowd.

"Fine."

I brought the cup up to my mouth, the strong scent of the rum filling my nose. I tried to down it with one big gulp, but it sat in my mouth too long and my throat and lungs gave a little spasm, pushing some of it back up, out of my mouth and nose. Some of it landed in the cup, but a fine mist sprayed out in all directions. The rum was now dripping from the sides of my mouth and nose. I didn't have a towel nearby, so I pulled my shirt up to my face to try and wipe it off. Trying not to look as pathetic as I thought I did, I made a second attempt at what was remaining in the cup and put it down on the coffee table.

They were all laughing loudly.

Coughing like mad from my now burning throat, I brought my hand up to wipe the rum off my face that the shirt hadn't gotten. I couldn't help but look down to the cup and the floor. I tried not to make eye contact with them.

"Dude, do you not know how to drink a shot?" Brandon asked between laughs.

"Yeah, it's just shitty rum," I lied, face and nose now burning since I essentially sneezed hard alcohol into my brain.

"Bullshit, JKYS. Go fill up your cup again," he said, pointing to the table.

There it was again. What the fuck did JKYS mean?

"No, I'm good," I said desperately, trying not to cough between the words coming out of my mouth.

"What's with JKYS? What the fuck does it mean? You say that shit a lot," I asked.

Brandon laughed.

"Are you serious? You don't get out much, do you? It means *just kill yourself*, fucktard."

What an ass.

"Either you fill it up, or we'll make you do a double shot," Brandon said, upping the threat.

Getting up from the couch, I grabbed the cup off the coffee table and walked over to the bottles. I felt dizzy now from the coughing, barely able to breathe out of my burning nose. The rum bottle was empty, leaving whiskey and gin. I felt like I'd heard someone say to stay with the same color when you're drinking, so I poured the last bit of the whiskey bottle into my cup and walked back to the couch.

I wanted to leave.

I wanted to dunk my head underwater to get this rum off of my face and out of my mouth and nose.

I just wanted out.

Brandon, laughing now reduced to heavy breathing to replace the oxygen he threw out at my expense, reached down

72

and grabbed his cup off the table and raised it. "A toast!" he said forcefully.

All the guys grabbed their cups and raised them.

"To Crazy Jake, and Tyler's first shot!" he barked.

The other three repeated the toast before drinking from their raised cups.

I pretended to drink, bringing the cup up to my closed mouth. My throat was still burning from the rum. The even stronger scent of the whiskey almost made me gag when it hit my nose. The last thing I wanted was to add more fuel to the fire.

After putting the cup down on the table, mixing it with a dozen other cups already there in the hopes they didn't find it still with the whiskey inside, I leaned back and pulled my phone out of my pocket. I wiped my hand on my shirt to get the remaining rum off before texting Luke.

Tyler: *Can you come pick me up? Please...*
I put the phone on my thigh, hoping for a quick response. After a couple minutes of listening to the guys joke about Mr. Hunter, the phone vibrated on my leg.

Luke: *Can it be later? We are still going.*

Tyler: *Please.*

Not taking my eyes off the phone now, I waited for his response.

Luke: *Okay, fine. I'll be there in about twenty minutes.*

While the guys kept talking, I sat there browsing my social feed on my phone. I found Jake in Spencer's follower list and browsed through some of his posts. He didn't seem crazy. They were pretty normal posts, and he was smiling in almost all of them. He had just posted a lot of pictures with a small group of girls a few hours ago. He wasn't doing anything with any of them or anything, so I don't think any were his girlfriend, but he just seemed to be around them a lot. It was weird. He wasn't a particularly good-looking guy. Not enough to have that many girls around him.

Man, what was I doing wrong? Here I was surrounded by guys I didn't really like, and he was out with half a dozen hot girls...

After about thirty minutes, I could just barely hear Luke's car whining as it made its way up the driveway. I shoved my phone into my pocket. I didn't have the patience to wait for Luke to text that he was here and stood up from the couch.

"My brother's here to pick me up. I'll see you guys later," I said, a little forced. I must have not realized how much of a lightweight I was, because standing up after thirty minutes and trying to balance didn't work so well. I could feel myself swaying a little side to side. I wasn't drunk, or at least I didn't think I was. I didn't exactly have something to reference this to. I was just swaying a little.

I didn't think this was what being drunk was.

I tried to control it so the guys wouldn't notice. I could just imagine the jokes now. "One Shot Tyler."

"All right, get out of here. We're out of booze for you to not drink anyway," Brandon snarkily responded.

"See you later," Spencer added. The other guys just sat without responding.

Walking out the double doors to the pool house, I realized that most of the guys were already gone. I was jealous. If I'd have known I could have left earlier, maybe I'd have gotten away without the rum shot. But it was too late now.

I hadn't seen them leave. None of them drove yet; we were a year away from being old enough to drive. So, they must have been picked up by someone. I didn't think anyone else had a sibling who could drive, so their parents must have picked them up.

How did they hide being drunk? They had to smell like alcohol and act like they'd been drinking. Maybe their parents just didn't care? I doubted that.

As I walked around the pathway that had led me to the pool earlier, I obsessed about this situation. How the hell had they left without me noticing, and who had picked them up? I don't know why it mattered, but it did for some reason.

I rounded the last bend in the walkway to see Tyler's car stopped right where he'd dropped me off, headlights shining directly at me. Looking down at the ground to avoid being blinded, I walked over to the passenger-side door. I was so happy to see that ugly piece of crap with wheels. It was my escape.

I climbed into the seat and just collapsed. Almost like the other guys had on the couches earlier. As if I'd just run a marathon, and this was the moment I passed the finish line and could stop running.

"You survived," Luke said, for the thousandth time this week, as he shifted the car back into gear.

"Barely," I said, too tired to explain it all.

Luke laughed. "Well, you must have had fun. I could smell the alcohol as soon as you sat down. How much did you drink?"

I really didn't want to explain what had happened. It was embarrassing. But I also didn't want him to think I got wasted. That wasn't me. But I had to say something...

"Not a lot. I'm not drunk. I guess I spilled a little on my shirt, which smells," I said, reaching down, pinching my shirt, and pulling it up to my nose.

It reeked.

"Well, no way you are getting past Mom and Dad smelling like that. Do you have another shirt or something?" he asked with a grin.

My jacket! As Luke started the drive down the hillside driveway, I awkwardly yanked my shirt off over my head, nearly punching the car ceiling. Once it was free, I threw it down to the floor by my feet and pulled on my hoodie over my head and onto my bare torso.

"Just don't breathe directly toward them when we get there. You'll probably be fine," he said, still grinning.

"So, how was it? Besides the alcohol bath," Luke asked.

"It was fine. We just hung out and messed around." I wanted to leave it at that. But there was no way he was going to leave it alone. My first high school party, my first attempt at drinking… He was going to want details.

"You suck at explaining things. Come on, man. Details."

"We just had some drinks and hung out in the pool house. Some guys swam in the pool, and a few others dicked around on the tennis court. But I just hung out."

"Alone?" he asked with a chuckle. "Come on, this was your chance to make friends. I hope you didn't avoid everyone and make it awkward by being the silent guy in the corner."

"No! I was normal."

I lied.

"They were in and out of the pool house and a few of us hung out and talked for the last hour or so."

"So, what do rich freshmen up here talk about?" he asked with some genuine curiosity.

"Not much. Brandon is a bit of a dick. But I already knew that."

"Yeah, I got that vibe from him watching your practice. Well, when you're this rich, I guess you don't need to be nice to people for them to still want to hang out with you," he said.

"Yeah. I guess so," I said, with a hint of jealousy in my voice. "I found out someone on our team is crazy. Do you know Jake on JV? I don't know his last name."

"I don't think so. What do you mean he's crazy?" Luke now had a confused or skeptical look on his face.

"He's on a ton of meds. Might have tried to kill himself or something," I said with a little bit of judgment in my tone. "Who does that? You must be pretty bad off to need meds for something like that."

"Who told you that? Jake?" Luke asked, his grin now completely gone and brow furrowed.

"No, Jake wasn't there. Brandon found out."

"Brandon? The guy you just called a dick? Sounds like a reliable source," he said.

I don't know why he was questioning this. Why did it matter?

"I don't know. But it feels weird knowing someone like that. It's weird having someone on meds like that play on my team."

"Why?" Luke asked sincerely. "You're surrounded by guys on ADD medication all day."

"Yeah, but ADD meds aren't for people who slit wrists," I said with a little laugh.

Luke wasn't laughing.

"I don't know if it's true, but even if it is, you can't laugh at this shit, Tyler. You don't know him well enough. Hell, you don't even know his last name, but you can laugh at him for taking medication? It could be from something that happened to him that you don't know about. Some people have had fucked up lives, and whatever it is, it's probably not his fault."

I just sat there in silence as the car hummed along the road home. I didn't know what to say back. Why was he being so weird about this?

After a nearly endless awkward silence, Luke jumped back in. "Look. You shouldn't give a shit if someone is taking medication. And if they are, that isn't something you should judge them for. Okay?"

"Fine," I said, now embarrassed but also mad that he got mad at me. I wasn't the one who'd said it first. Brandon was.

We sat in silence the rest of the ride home. After Luke parked, we walked up to the house. It felt even smaller than before. After seeing Brandon's house, this one felt like the crank on the vise that was squeezing its narrow stature had a few extra spins while I was gone.

Thankfully, my parents weren't in the entryway. So, I made my way quickly up to the bathroom Luke and I shared to try and shower off the rum before I went to bed.

I loved showers.

I could step into the box with running warm water spraying over my body that drowned out the sounds around me and feel incredibly relaxed. The water flowed down my head and face, removing any sign of the rum from my cheeks, and continued down my chest to do the same.

I could stand there for hours. This was my space suit. No one else was around. I didn't have to worry about anything. I could just stand there and feel the water cover my body, washing off what the day had left on me and leaving me fresh.

I walked into the shower scarred by the day, and I walked out myself again. If I could take a hundred showers a day, I would. I felt like I needed that reset all day long.

After drying off, I went to my room and slipped under my bedsheets. The coldness of the sheets not yet warmed by my body felt amazing on my bare skin.

It took a while to relax. I could still feel the music from the party in my head. Not really hear it; my bedroom was silent. But I could still feel the strain my head was putting on itself from the stress of it all.

After about fifteen minutes, I could feel the bed warm to match my body temperature. My head gradually settled down to almost a calm state, and I slowly slipped off to sleep.

7

There were very few things that made both four-year-old and fourteen-year-old Tyler excited. I increasingly avoided mud puddles, clowns, and coloring books as time went on. But two things stood out as being amazingly awesome at both ages.

Lego sets and dogs.

If I could have a puppy that knew how to assemble Lego bricks, I'd be in heaven. Since that was probably impossible, I'd happily settle for a puppy asleep in a bed next to me while I built something.

Luke used to love Lego building too. It was one of the only things I remember from when I was young. But when I was really little, I would sit there and watch him building something super complex, something that had a lot of joints, color coordination, size, and an instruction manual as thick as a textbook.

I'd sit there trying to do the same but was barely able to assemble anything that represented a structure that could tangibly exist in reality.

They obviously were a choking hazard and hard to hold for little kids, so before my first Lego set, I had Duplos. Duplos were huge versions of Lego bricks. Where a Lego piece could be a half inch to one inch long, Duplos were easily four or five times larger. At that age, I didn't care that they weren't "real" Lego bricks. I was just glad to have something that looked like what Luke was playing with.

I loved solo Lego sets. I could open up the boxes, sort the bags by instruction book step, and place them in little bowls, making the pieces easier to find. I could build for hours, each task set forth in the instruction manual guiding my process.

Yes, it was super tedious and was akin to assembling IKEA furniture, but I loved it. I could relax, occupy my mind, and have something to show for it when I was done.

If I had an office job in twenty or thirty years where I wore a suit and carried a briefcase, I'd still go home and play Legos on weekends to decompress.

I was sure of it.

With all the stress and pressure I'd been feeling from moving, starting at a new school, and playing with a new team, I really needed to decompress. Normally, I'd run to the store and find a Lego set I hadn't built yet and spend a day watching a stupid movie and building. But this weekend I had plans.

My dad said that a coworker's dog had puppies a couple months ago and they were looking for homes. He agreed to take one and drove out to their house to pick it up while my mom and I went to buy supplies.

We needed everything. Food, bed, leashes and collars, toys… I wanted everything.

Who didn't love puppies? Crazy people, evil people, people I didn't trust…

I don't care if you're "not a dog person." If you don't think a puppy is fun or cute, you're a broken human being. Big dogs can be an acquired taste, but puppies? Puppies are for everyone.

After grabbing everything we needed, I rushed to the car and threw it into the trunk before jumping into the passenger seat. I wanted to get home as fast as we could. I needed to set up his things before my dad brought him home.

It had been a few weeks since they'd agreed to let me get a dog, and I had been obsessing about it constantly. You know those cool guys who walked around with their dog off leash and the dog was hanging, just as cool as the owner? Where they seemed to have some special communication method that facilitated some sort of symbiotic relationship? And they could go outside and have hot girls swarm them to pet the perfect four-legged wingman?

Yeah.

I wanted to be that guy so badly.

When we got home, my dad's car was already in the driveway. Damn, didn't beat him home. I was a little disappointed that I couldn't prep the house in time, but that feeling went away almost instantly, replaced with pure excitement.

I tried to stay cool and walk from the car to the house, but my speed walk made my mom laugh behind me.

"In a hurry?" she said to me as I powered up the cracked concrete path to the front door. I didn't have to turn around to tell she had a big grin on her face. You could tell by her tone.

"No. Why?" I asked, trying to seem like it was no big deal.

"Bull... Go. I'm sure your dad's excited to introduce you two. He's been talking about this damn dog every night."

My hands were full of bags of dog supplies, so I used my shoulder and pushed the front door a little too forcefully. It slammed the inner handle hard on the little rubber protector mounted on the wall behind it.

I rushed through the entryway and down the hall to drop the bags on the living room couch. When I turned around, my dad was walking toward me from the front of the house. He must have been upstairs.

He wasn't smiling and I didn't see a dog. What the hell? What was going on?

"Hey, Tyler," he said, with a serious tone.

"So, it turns out they wanted to keep the puppy. I'm sorry."

"What? Why?"

"I don't know, I guess they just liked him so much that they weren't able to part ways. Why don't you go upstairs and drop the supplies in your room. We can go search for a puppy next weekend at a rescue group they recommended. I'm sorry."

Damnit. Really? This was fucked. I was too sad to be outwardly angry, but I was still angry. After begrudgingly grabbing the bags I had just moments before thrown onto the couch from excitement and joy, I slowly made my way upstairs, chin down to my chest and staring at every step as I made my way up.

This sucked.

I opened the door to my bedroom much less enthusiastically than I had the front door to the house. As my body pushed past the hinged barrier and entered the room, I dropped the bags at my feet. Taking a step toward my bed, I lifted my chin just enough to see that something was already on it.

A box.

It had *Tyler's Things* written on its side in what was clearly my dad's handwriting.

Really? Right now? I didn't want to put more shit away right now. I felt like we had been moving in for years.

I just wanted to lie down in my bed for a while. I grabbed the box to move it to the floor and felt it move, like its contents shifted to the opposite side. I hadn't tilted it. What? Was my old junior water polo ball in here?

I put it on the floor and lifted the top to look inside and was instantly greeted with *huge* light brown eyes and an equally huge yawn.

"What? Are you serious?!" I couldn't hold it in.

I reached in and picked up the small brown puppy, now fully awake after my outburst.

"I think this qualifies as the best prank I've ever pulled on you." My dad was now standing in the open doorway to my room.

"You dick," I said, but with a massive smile on my face. I was too happy to be actually angry.

"Hey, that's not what you say to a guy who gets you a dog. In some cultures, you'd owe me for life after doing something like that."

I was too busy with the puppy to respond to him. I held him close to my chest with my left arm and hand underneath. I held my right hand up to his nose in a fist so he could get used to my smell. Every time he sniffed, I slowly petted his head before bringing my hand back in front of him.

After a few times, instead of sniffing, he licked me. He was so calm!

"How is he this chill? I'd be freaking out after being taken out of a box by a strange giant," I asked.

"They said that he was the quietest of the litter. When people came to pick up the others, they got super playful, so they were picked first. He isn't really a runt. Same size as the rest of 'em. But he's just calmer and quieter apparently. I figured that it made sense to get the socially awkward and quiet dog for the socially awkward and quiet kid."

Had to throw in a joke...

"He's been in that box for a little while. Why don't you take him for a walk?" he added.

"Yeah, good idea," I said, scrambling through the shopping bags to find the leash and collar we had bought just thirty minutes before. I hoped we got the right size! He was tiny.

I pulled out the black collar we'd bought. It was a special one I'd researched before we went to the store that would prevent puppies from escaping if they tried to pull themselves out backwards. It was a normal collar, not a choke chain, that would tighten slightly when he pulled back instead of tightening all the way and hurting him.

I was terrified of choking him and making him hate me. Eyeballing it, I loosened the straps to what felt like a reasonable length and snapped it on him.

Within half a second, he looked down, and with a quick swipe of his right paw, it slid off his head and onto the ground.

Maybe I should tighten it a little.

After a quick adjustment, it was back on him and immune to his swipes. I then clicked on the leash clip and stood up from the floor, holding my end. He instantly jumped up and started running to the door. When he reached the end of the leash, he snapped back so hard he almost fell over.

"Slow down. I'm coming," I said in a calm voice, trying not to laugh.

We made our way past my dad, down the stairs, and out the front door. The leash was fully extended as he ran ahead of me at full speed. As soon as his paws touched grass, he squatted and pissed more liquid than his tiny body should have been able to hold.

How huge was this guy's bladder?

After what felt like a solid five minutes of pissing, (I might be exaggerating), we started our walk down the block. He had to smell everything he walked past, barked at every living thing that flew or scurried by, and peed a few more times.

We got back to the house about twenty minutes later and walked straight back upstairs. After pouring him some water to drink and leaving the bowl on the floor in the bathroom Luke and I shared, I made my way with him to my bedroom. I laid out his brand-new bed on the floor right next to my nightstand and put him in it.

I played with him for hours.

We opened all of his new toys and played with them all until he could barely keep his eyes open. When it became time for me to head off to bed, he was already passed out in his. And I swear he had as big of a smile as I did.

8

I spent every waking moment that weekend playing with my puppy. For some reason, I was having a hard time naming him. There were so many options, but nothing was good enough. So many seemed generic and didn't fit him. I had a feeling it was going to take me awhile to figure it out.

It was painful leaving him Monday morning to go to school. My mom was going to watch him while I was gone during the day, but I knew it would be hard to focus at school knowing that he was waiting for me at home. Telling myself that he'd be there when I got back never seemed to actually help, but I said it in my head anyway.

Every class was a blur. All I could do was count down the seconds to when I could go home and play with him.

Yes, I was obsessed.

When lunch came around, I texted my mom asking how he was doing as I dropped my things in my locker and grabbed the bag with my lunch in it.

Mom: *He peed in the living room and ate one of your polo bags. But other than that, he's alive.*

She texted me a picture of him sitting and looking up at the camera with an innocent look on his face, scraps of cloth from my bag strewn all about the floor behind and around him. He was so fucking cute I couldn't be mad.

Tyler: *Sorry. I'll clean it up when I get home.*

Mom: *I already cleaned it, don't worry. Do you have a name yet?*

Tyler: *Not yet. I'll figure one out soon.*

His destruction put a huge smile on my face. I don't know why, but I liked having this "problem" to deal with.

With my bag in hand, I made my way down to the lunch tables to find Spencer. I found him at one of the blue rubber-coated, metal-grated round tables that every school seemed to have these days. Chris and Nick were with him, flanking him on either side.

"What's up?" I asked casually while grabbing a seat on the free bench opposite Spencer.

"Absolutely nothing. Chris was telling me about his dad's new car, even though I've been begging him to stop. No one cares about his dad's mid-life crisis," Spencer said, jabbing at Chris with a light smile on his face. He could seem like a dick sometimes, but we all knew he was just joking around.

"Shut up, it's a cool car," Chris said, slightly mad, but still with a smile.

"Yeah, if you are on your third wife and have a comb-over," Nick said, now joining in on Spencer's digging.

"Whatever," Chris said, starting to get defeated.

Before I had a chance to open my lunch bag to pull out my sandwich, Brandon shot up behind me fast.

"Guys, come with me. Right now. You need to see this," he said, almost out of breath.

"We just sat down. Can it wait ten minutes?" Spencer said, sounding slightly annoyed.

"No. Get off your ass and come with me." Brandon was out of breath but had this devious smile on his face, like he was about to reveal a prank or something bad. It made me a little nervous.

"Fine," Spencer said with a frustrated tone as he stood up from the table.

As he stood up, the rest of us joined and we started follow a power-walking Brandon. He was trying to go so fast that he had to keep looking over his shoulder to make sure we were behind him.

"Come on!" he said, trying to get us to quicken our pace.

We made our way around one of the disconnected buildings that backed up to a hillside. Most of the buildings here were up against the hills surrounding the school, which gave it a nice oasis feeling due to the brown hills and carefully manicured lawns and greenery that made up the school grounds.

Brandon started to slow down and was slightly crouching as he walked toward the corner of the building, like he was about to sneak up on someone.

We all started to do the same, being quiet, but not knowing why.

The corner of the building had a small concrete bench that extended a few yards beyond where the wall ended and had a small planter behind it with small bushes sprouting up from it. Brandon, and then the rest of us, took a knee behind the bench and tried to look through the bushes to see what he was pointing at.

Jake was standing about twenty feet away with another guy I didn't recognize, and they were talking about something. They were almost whispering, so we couldn't hear everything. But all I could make out was "Not yet" and "I don't think they are ready. I don't think I'm ready to tell them." As he said that, he looked down at the ground like he was sad or embarrassed. Or both.

The other guy must have been a sophomore or older. I didn't recognize him from my classes or from polo.

He reached forward with his right hand and lightly raised Jake's head with a couple fingers under his chin, bringing his eyes up to his.

"I know. It's okay," he said with a smile.

And kissed him.

I could feel the guys next to me start to move around, probably from the adrenaline and excitement of what they'd just witnessed. Spencer was on my right; his eyes were big and his jaw was dropped. He was not expecting that either.

When I looked to the left, my heart stopped.

Brandon was filming this on his phone and had a huge smile on his face, eyes big like an evil mastermind.

What the fuck was he about to do?

I punched him in the shoulder, hoping he'd get the message and stop. This was not cool.

After a couple seconds, he stopped filming and looked back to us and nodded in the direction we'd come from.

"Go!" he mouthed silently to us.

We all turned back and started making our way around the front of the building.

When we got far enough away, Brandon exploded. "How fucking funny is that?"

He was so excited. It was scaring me. The other guys were too shocked to speak.

"What are you going to do with that video?" I asked seriously.

"What do you care? He's a fucking faggot. I can do whatever I want. JKYS," he said, matter-of-fact like.

"No you can't. That's fucked up. Delete it," I said, getting angry now.

"Shut up. I'll do what I want." He was now looking down at his phone, his evil grin widening...

"Fuck you," I said and started walking away. Nick and Chris stayed behind, looking somewhat amused. Spencer looked about to argue with Brandon for a second, then walked off to join me.

We made our way back to the lunch table and sat down. I sat there silently for a minute or so before asking Spencer, "What is he going to do?"

Spencer looked worried.

"He said he's going to use it to try to get Jake to quit the team, or else he will post it to his social media accounts."

"What? That's fucked up! We need to stop him," I said. My heart rate was now pounding, and I was really getting worried.

"Why the fuck would he do that?" I said, trying to come to grips with the fact that he was such a dick. "I fucking hate him."

"Yeah, it's not cool." Spencer looked upset too, but not nearly as much as I was.

"We need to do something. Please. He won't listen to me, but he might listen to you." I was begging now.

"I don't know, man. He is really serious about this." He was looking down at the table now, unable to make eye contact with me.

This was fucked up. I was so angry I couldn't eat.

The bell rang and everyone started to make their way back to class. I'd try to talk to Brandon at practice. I wouldn't see him until then and I hoped he wouldn't do anything stupid before then. Knowing him, this was a time bomb. No way he could sit on this for long.

I was terrified for Jake. I didn't care if you didn't like the guy, you didn't blackmail him by threatening to out him for being gay. That was next-level asshole.

I couldn't focus in my last class and was hoping the clock would run down faster so I could try to stop this. I didn't know how, but I needed to stop him.

If I told someone else to get help, I'd be the one outing Jake. In case Brandon didn't follow through, I didn't want to be the one to unnecessarily out him. I just didn't know what to do.

When class ended, I grabbed my bag from my locker and sped off to the pool, hoping to get there before Jake did. I rounded the corner to the pool deck entrance and rushed in.

I was too late…

Over by the corner where we usually got changed, I could see Brandon talking to Jake. As Brandon continued to speak, Jake looked more and more concerned.

Then Brandon pulled out his phone...

Jake looked at the screen and was suddenly frozen where he stood, terrified.

Brandon said a few more things that I couldn't hear, which resulted in Jake saying loudly, "Fuck you!"

Brandon smiled and chuckled. I could hear him say that fucking acronym again. "JKYS."

Coach overheard Jake's reaction and walked over to them. Brandon quickly put his phone into his pocket.

He looked like he was trying to find out what was going on, but they both looked tight-lipped. We had time before our practice started, but he seemed to tell them they needed to stay on the pool deck to calm down.

They went to opposite sides of the bleachers and sat down.

I was too scared to talk to Brandon. I wasn't able to stop him from talking to Jake, and I was terrified of what he would do next.

I dropped my stuff where I normally did, next to where they were arguing, and made my way to the bleachers. I decided to sit next to Jake. Maybe if Brandon saw me there, he'd realize that we weren't cool with this.

Jake didn't know I knew but seemed a little confused as to why I was there with him.

"What's up?" I asked, trying to sound normal and casual.

"Nothing. Can you please go? I want to be alone for a little bit," he said, sounding defeated.

"Um... okay. You sure?"

"Yeah, just go," he said, a little more seriously.

I stood up and made my way back to my bag to wait for practice. Varsity was just getting into the pool, so I had an hour or so before our practice started, but I didn't want to be near Brandon.

I'd missed my chance to fix this.

When it came time to suit up for practice, everyone made their way to our normal corner and started getting changed. Jake wouldn't make eye contact with anyone. I don't know if he knew that anyone else knew, but he looked beyond embarrassed.

Just as we were about to jump in the pool, I saw Brandon take his phone out of his rolled-up pants. With that fucked-up grin on his face, he tapped the screen a few times before putting it back in his pants pocket and rolling them back up.

He didn't. He wouldn't...

I reached down to find my phone to check social media to see if he posted it, but Coach came around to us right then.

"Guys, stop messing around with your phones and get in the pool. You have twenty minutes to warm up. If you aren't in the pool in thirty seconds, it's going to be in-and -outs for an hour instead of a scrimmage," he said, visibly frustrated and looking directly at Brandon and me.

That was the longest practice of my life. I couldn't see what he'd done for two full hours. It was killing me. I couldn't imagine what Jake felt like. I don't know if he'd seen Brandon pull out his phone from his pants. If he had, he must have been beyond terrified.

After what seemed like four hours, practice came to an end. I scrambled over to my bag and dried my hands as fast as I could before pulling out my phone.

It was dead.

Fuck. The battery was always low about this time if I left it on all day, but it usually had some left. The heat from the sun on my black bag must have shut it off to prevent overheating.

I changed as fast as I could with my improving deck changing skills, grabbed my things, and ran off to where Luke had parked that morning.

He was sitting in the car, distracted by listening to some Iron Maiden on full blast, and looked a little startled when I yanked the passenger door open and jumped in.

"Let's go," I said, out of breath and with pool water soaking through my shirt. I was in such a hurry that I hadn't dried myself off completely.

"You're in a hurry. What's up?" He laughed as he asked.

"Can we just go home? I don't want to talk about it right now."

"Okay, okay," he said, confused. He stopped asking questions and turned down the music a bit before driving off.

When we got home, I rushed out of the car so fast I left the passenger door open, which Luke closed as he made his way up to the house. I ran inside and sprinted upstairs to my room to plug in my phone. It was still dead but should be cool enough to recharge and turn on now.

I threw open my bedroom door, went straight to my bedside table, and connected the power cable that was plugged into the wall behind my bed.

The phone's logo flashed on the screen for a moment before showing the battery-charging animation. I quickly hit the power button and waited for the home screen to appear. I had thirty text messages waiting for me. I skipped past them, already knowing what they might be about, and opened up my social feed.

Right at the top of my feed was exactly what I had feared.

I was too angry to read the over two hundred comments that were underneath the video and hit the power button on the side, turning the screen black before falling to the floor with my knees to my chest.

I wrapped my arms around my knees and just sat there.

I didn't know what to do, who to talk to, or what I would even say to them.

I just needed to sit there.

I felt so bad for Jake.

I cried.

After a few minutes, I started to feel a little calmer. I had just wiped my face clean when Luke knocked on my door and opened it, not waiting for me to invite him in.

He was holding the puppy as he walked in.

"Dude, what's going on? Something must be totally fucked. You didn't even check on this little guy when you got home. Did someone die?" he asked, genuinely concerned. No jokes. Just concern.

"No, just something Brandon did to Jake on our team. That guy that I told you about after the party."

"What did he do?" he asked calmly.

I grabbed my phone and unlocked it. The post was still on the screen. I handed the phone to Luke and just sat there in silence as he watched it.

His eyes got bigger as the video went on, then narrowed into one of the angriest faces I've ever seen on him. It scared me a little.

"What. The. Fuck," he said, clearly out of words.

"Why the fuck would Brandon post this? He's such a fucking asshole!" He was getting more and more angry as he spoke.

Luke closed the door and put the puppy on the floor next to me. Tail wagging, the puppy jumped into my lap and put his paws on my chest, trying to climb up toward my face. I wrapped my hands around him and petted him slowly from the top of his head down his back. Over and over again.

Luke stopped talking and sat on my bed. We didn't talk much after that. He sat there for a few more minutes before heading downstairs.

I skipped dinner and just walked the puppy before heading to bed. I overheard Luke talking to our parents about it, and I was thankful that he said that he thought I needed a little space. They didn't ask me about it and let me be. I didn't want to explain it to them. I didn't want anyone to know that I hadn't been able to prevent it from happening.

I didn't know if I'd be able to sleep, but I had to try. Tomorrow was not going to be easy, I could tell already.

9

Thankfully, I was able to get a few hours of sleep before I had to get up for school. I walked the puppy down the block before I dropped him back at home and grabbed my backpack. Luke and I drove over to school like usual. He put on some music, and we didn't talk much. We were both normally pretty quiet in the mornings.

Something was off when we got to school. There were groups of people talking to each other quietly all over the place.

I tried to ignore them and walked to my locker to get my books for Mr. Hunter's class.

When I got to the room, there was a substitute teacher in the room and the rest of the class was starting to make their way to their seats. They were all chatting amongst themselves seriously. No one seemed to have a smile on their face.

When I sat down in my chair, the substitute looked down at the seating chart and back up to me. She walked over to me and asked, "Are you Tyler?"

"Yeah, is something wrong?" I asked back.

"Mr. Hunter is meeting the rest of your water polo team in the gym. Here is a pass," she said, handing me a small piece of paper that granted me permission to leave class. "Go ahead and head down there. Take your things with you just in case it lasts longer than the class period."

"Do you know what it's about?" I asked nervously.

"Mr. Hunter can explain when you get down there," she said, avoiding the question.

I grabbed my things and made my way down to the gym.

As I walked, I could feel my heart pounding faster and faster. Was I in trouble? What did they know? Did Brandon try to blame the rest of us?

I tried to run through every scenario in my mind as I made the long walk down to the gym. It was a huge building that housed the basketball court and a ton of bleacher seating. The school used it for assemblies all the time since it was one of the few indoor places that could hold a lot of people.

As I walked in the main double doors, I could see all my teammates in the bleachers to the left, talking amongst themselves. Mr. Hunter, the school principal, Mr. Sobek, and a woman I didn't recognize were off talking by the basketball hoop to the right of me. They were quietly talking to each other, but Mr. Hunter paused to look up at me when I entered the room.

He looked terrible.

Something was really wrong.

"Go grab a seat, Tyler," he said and tried to put a welcoming smile on his face but failed.

I nodded back at him and made my way up to the empty bench seat next to Luke.

After a few more minutes, the rest of the team made their way in and sat down. There was a soft crowd mumble all around as the conversation and news of the video clearly made its rounds and found everyone.

"He didn't... Did he? This has to be a joke," I heard from my right.

"Has anyone seen Brandon? What a shit. I hope he burns," I heard from my left.

I didn't see Brandon anywhere.

Spencer was on the far side of the bleachers but avoided eye contact with me.

Mr. Hunter and the other adults started to walk over to the sideline near where we were all sitting, and the crowd went silent.

Mr. Hunter was looking down at his feet as he walked up. After a few seconds, he lifted his head and began to speak.

"I wish I could stand here and say 'good morning' to everyone. It pains me dearly to not be able to say that today." He paused for a few seconds before continuing.

"As some of you may have already heard, Jake Waller passed away late last night."

He paused again. The room was all quiet now. No one knew how to react.

"We can't provide any details at this time out of respect for Jake and his family. But we felt it was important to bring you all in here to tell you, instead of having you all find out by other means.

"At this time, please do your absolute best to hold speculation to a minimum. As details emerge, and with permission from his family, we will share them with you. But until then, guessing and rumors won't help anything."

My heart sank straight down to my feet at the sudden realization that he might have killed himself after what had happened yesterday.

I put my hand on Luke's thigh for support as I leaned forward a little. I felt dizzy.

Luke put his arm around my back and put his hand on my shoulder. His silent support helped give me the ability to look back up and keep listening to Mr. Hunter.

"Mr. Sobek has given permission for anyone here to go home to be with your families today. He will be sending an email to them as soon as we are done talking to explain the situation."

"Dr. Becker," he said, gesturing to the woman I didn't recognize. "Dr. Becker is the school district's head counselor, and has taken up a temporary office here on campus in the admin building near Mr. Sobek."

She walked forward a bit and sent a kind nod in our direction.

"I encourage everyone here to visit with her. She is here to help us all, including myself, work through this difficult time. Even if it's just a quick twenty-minute check-in, please do it. It will be very difficult for a little while, but there are people here who can help. No one is too tough to get help every once in a while. I will be speaking with her at length today, and I encourage you all to follow."

He turned to Dr. Becker, and she handed him a thick bundle of what looked like business cards.

He walked over to the far left and handed the pile to the person in the front row before walking back to where he stood before.

"Please take one of these and pass it down the line. Dr. Becker will be here for the next few weeks. You all have permission to visit her office any time during the school day. All you need to do is to ask your teacher if you can use the restroom and show them this card. They will grant you permission to leave class and head to her office, no questions asked.

"Out of respect for Jake and his family, we ask that you avoid discussing this on social media. It is time for us all to come together and show our support for them during what is the most earth-shattering and difficult time in their lives. Jake was a wonderful kid. He was quiet, which made him a little misunderstood, but those who knew him well liked and appreciated him. Please keep the best of him in your thoughts and hearts, and I promise we will all get through this. Mr. Sobek, do you have anything to add?"

Mr. Hunter stepped back to stand with Dr. Becker as Mr. Sobek started to talk.

99

"Thank you, Mr. Hunter," he said, with a somewhat serious look on his face. He didn't appear to be as emotionally distraught as Mr. Hunter, but that's probably because he hadn't known Jake personally.

"The next several weeks will be very hard for everyone. It will be hard to focus on school, practice, and life in general. We want it to be as clear as possible that you are not alone, and we are here to help you. In addition to Dr. Becker, we have a lot of resources to help you all through times like this. If you feel like you need additional assistance with anything, please reach out to me, Dr. Becker, Mr. Hunter, or any other staff member you feel comfortable speaking with at this school. We will all do our best to help get you what you need to get through this.

"Before I hand off to Dr. Becker to help answer questions, you are all free to stay in here until the class period is over before rejoining your classmates or going home. I would also like to reinforce what Mr. Hunter said. I strongly suggest that you set aside some time in the next few days to speak with Dr. Becker. Please take advantage of all the resources we have at our disposal. We want to help you any way we can.

"In my email to your parents, I will include links and phone numbers to many of these resources for you to seek outside of school hours as well. There are phone numbers available to call twenty-four seven, outside counselors in the area with special training for situations like this, and support groups where you can go together and talk through things. All of these resources are free of charge to you, thanks to a hefty anonymous donation made this morning.

"Dr. Becker, Mr. Hunter, and I will stay here with you to help answer any questions you may have. If you don't have any questions, please either stay here quietly so we can hear and answer everything we can or, if you need to talk amongst each other, please do so outside."

I think everyone was too shocked to ask questions. Dr. Becker stepped forward and tried to extract some from us all, but it was silent every time she stopped talking.

Turning to Luke, I asked if we could go outside. As big as that gym was, with its high ceilings and large open air, it was claustrophobic. I needed to breathe. But I didn't want to go outside alone.

"Sure, let's go. Do you want to talk to Coach or Dr. Becker first? You were really beat up yesterday before you knew everything. I'm worried that this will be even harder."

"No, I'm okay right now. I don't know what I would even talk to them about," I said, sounding exhausted. Putting words together felt like work. Speaking quietly and slowly helped me process what I was saying.

"Okay, let me check in with Coach and I'll meet you outside," Luke said as we stood up and made our way down the wooden extendable staircase leading up the bleachers.

I walked toward the doors and pushed them open with both arms, using my body to lean into it. I felt too weak to muscle them open using just my arms.

Even with all of that effort, they felt almost like someone had duct-taped them closed because the first few inches took more effort than they should have.

The sun hit my face with noticeable heat and I squinted as I walked outside. There was a four-foot-tall chain-link fence directly in front of the entrance to the gym, separating the access road from a small ravine with a creek that spanned the length of the small valley the school was in.

I walked up to it and leaned on the top galvanized bar while looking down at the minuscule amount of water flowing through it. The way the water would hit a rock, swirl, then take a new direction to keep flowing downhill was mesmerizing. Even the smallest amount of water found its way around even the largest rock, eventually.

It seemed so simple down there. Water, rock, dirt, and vegetation, interacting with each other in their own way, yet still behaving predictably. Water flowed downhill, rocks provided structure, dirt moved with the flow of water and fed the vegetation that grew upwards toward sunlight.

Thinking back to that first class with Mr. Hunter, when he talked about the supernova and how studying it meant learning about the tiniest of neutrinos and the largest of stars and galaxies, I felt like I could dissect the creek the same way. I tried to imagine why water always behaved in ways that made predictable waves and spinning jetties as it interacted with surfaces it impacted, and how the plants along the bank would take that water and use it to grow and live by defying gravity to bring water up through their stems to the highest branches.

I tried to imagine the individual dirt particles, smaller than a grain of sand breaking off from the rest and floating down the creek to a new location. One by one, they'd flow down until the ravine itself grew wider and wider as more and more earth was moved. Years, decades, centuries… A lot of change happening on the small level, but only noticeable after a lot of time had passed.

Maybe a rock would fall off a cliff wall, making a big splash while bringing a cascade of dirt down with it, which would speed things up. But those wouldn't be all the time. Maybe they were far enough apart that it didn't make that much of a difference in the grand scheme, but to the dirt, it would feel enormous.

Luke walked up behind me and put a hand on the back of my head before annoyingly tousling my hair.

"Want to go home, or do you want to stay here today?" he asked.

"Let's go home."

We made our way to his car, after less than an hour since we were in it last, and started to drive home.

"Can you help explain it to Mom and Dad? I don't want to talk about it with them yet. I just want some privacy," I said. I was just too tired to talk about it right now.

"Yeah, of course," he said in his normal supportive tone. "But I think you should talk to someone about it. Doesn't have to be me or Mom and Dad, but try not to hold it in. I think Coach would be a good place to start. He seems to know you well enough and he seems to have a level head on his shoulders. I'm surprised he was the one who told us today and not Mr. Sobek. Seems like something a principal should do."

"I don't know. Maybe because it was his player and we're his team. I'll think about it," I said, hoping that he wouldn't pressure me.

He didn't.

Mom was out of the house when we got home. Maybe she'd gone grocery shopping or something. The puppy was in a small plastic crate with a bed and water bowl inside. He was destroying a toy we got him that was supposed to be indestructible. He had some sharp teeth and determination.

I got him out of the kennel and put his leash on him. After a quick walk up and down the block, we went up to my room and played a bit. I was so tired that I ended up falling asleep on the floor with him. For the first time in a while, my mind was blank. Maybe it was too much to process, or I was just shutting down. Either way, my mind faded to black and I slept without dreaming.

My phone was turned off. I didn't want to talk to anyone else. So, I ended up sleeping for almost three hours. I think that was the longest I'd slept during the day in years.

When I woke, the puppy was lying curled up in my armpit, with his head resting on my chest.

He must have woken at the same time, because he was looking right at my face as I lifted my head to look down toward him. There was no way that he knew what was going on, but I could almost see concern in his face. Maybe I was projecting that and saw what I wanted, or needed, to see. But I could almost swear it was there.

Luke came in to check on me when he heard me moving around again. He said he'd spoken to Mom and said I could stay up here if I wanted to. No pressure.

He brought up dinner to me to eat in my room and walked with me when I took the puppy out again. He didn't try to talk to me or ask questions. He just walked in silence.

He just knew how to read people. He knew how to help me feel comfortable.

10

At school the next day, all the teachers tried to make it feel as normal as possible. Classes had regular assignments, the normal drama continued, but no adult spoke about what had happened.

The other students were still in full rumor and conjecture mode, but the teachers tried not to join in.

By now, it had leaked from the family that Jake killed himself, confirming my deepest fear.

His dad had found him unconscious in his bed after overdosing on a sleep medication he had. The paramedics had taken him to the hospital, but he was already dead. I guess the pills made him sleep so deeply that his breathing slowed to nothing, and he'd died from lack of oxygen.

I didn't know if that was a good or bad way to go. I'd imagine you wouldn't know, being asleep. But when you were sleeping, your brain was still working. It must have felt that it was slowly dying and was probably screaming out in pain but was unable to wake him up to breathe.

I couldn't stop thinking about what he'd felt like.

Had he felt anything or everything?

I didn't even know if there was a middle ground.

It was terrifying and made me feel sick all day.

When lunch came around, I couldn't sit out at the tables in the quad. I needed to get away from all the conversation and the rumors. I couldn't handle it right now.

I made my way up to Mr. Hunter's room, hoping he'd let me eat in there, away from other people.

He'd understand.

When I opened the door to his room, he was sitting at the long desk at the front near his computer, eating in silence.

Maybe we were trying to do the same thing.

He looked up to me as I entered and tried to smile.

"Hey, Mr. Hunter. Is it okay if I eat in here today?" I asked quietly and almost out of breath. Thinking about how Jake felt got me so worked up I felt like I was about to crash.

"Of course. Please," he said after swallowing the food he had in his mouth.

"How are you doing?" he asked casually. "I was talking with Luke yesterday, and he was saying that you were having a hard time with this. More so than he was expecting. Is there anything you wanted to talk about?"

"No… I don't know," I said as I dropped my stuff at my normal desk. I knew that I didn't need to sit there since this wasn't normal class. But it was familiar.

"From what it sounded like, you had a very strong reaction to the video being posted. More so than some of the others who saw it. I didn't know you were so close to Jake."

I slowly opened up the brown paper bag that contained my lunch that my mom had made for me this morning. I pulled out a small plastic bag with a turkey sandwich inside. There was a small Post-it Note on the bag for me with a note written in my mom's handwriting.

Always remember… You are braver than you believe, stronger than you seem, and smarter than you think.
—Christopher Robin to Winnie the Pooh

106

I looked at it for a few seconds, rereading it before putting it down.

"I always saw you around Spencer, Nick, Chris, and Brandon. Were you two friends off the pool deck?" he asked, trying to poke and prod again.

"No, we weren't close or anything."

"Hmm," Mr. Hunter said with a little nod to acknowledge my answer.

"I don't know. I just felt bad for him. That really sucked."

"It did. It must have been hard to see that post come from one of your friends," he said as he grabbed his lunch and walked over to sit across from me at the tall lab table I was eating at.

"Brandon isn't my friend," I said angrily. I hated that he'd said that.

"I wish he didn't post that video…. I just wish none of this happened."

"I know, me too," he said to me with a genuine sadness in his tone.

I was starting to get angry at the thought of Brandon. I hated him so much.

"I just don't understand it. I don't get any of it… Why would Brandon do this? Why would Jake kill himself?" My words were speeding up and I was getting visibly agitated.

After a few seconds of near silence, my heavy breathing audible, Mr. Hunter reached into his bag and pulled out a small bag and held it up.

"Do you like pistachios? My wife keeps buying them, but I'm too lazy to break open the shells for small pieces of food. Call me crazy, but eating food is about gaining energy, not expelling it."

"No… thanks…" I said as my breathing began to slow with the momentary distraction.

"Why do you think he did it?" he asked. He emphasized the *you* to make it sound like he'd already formulated his own opinion but was curious about mine.

I must have been quiet for a while because he said "Don't worry, this is just between us. I promise."

"I don't know. He hated Jake for some reason. He treated him like shit ever since he found out he was in therapy for something... and when he found out he was also gay, Brandon had even more ammo."

I paused for a second and just stared down at my sandwich. I hadn't taken a bite yet. I just held it in both my hands in front of me.

"I didn't know he was homophobic, but it doesn't surprise me. He's an asshole... Sorry." I tried to recover from that last comment.

"It's okay. I understand how you might feel," he said, in a supportive and nonjudgmental tone.

"I just don't know *why* he would do it. I knew he *could* do it. Brandon's a jerk. Like, I knew he was capable of it. But I just don't get *why*."

I paused, not sure if I should tell him this, but...

"Brandon used to say 'JKYS' to people all the time," I said cautiously.

"What does that mean?" Mr. Hunter asked genuinely.

"Just go kill yourself... or something," I said, pretending not to know it intimately.

Mr. Hunter sat there in shock for a few seconds.

"Wow," he said in pure disbelief. "Maybe, in time, we will find answers to what was going through his head. But I'm sure it's a complex thing. At your age, there are a lot of emotions and feelings that you face every day and for a lot of things. You just don't have the control skills yet to handle them. At your age there are a lot of fights, short but strong relationships, a lot of impulsive responses and reactions to things... It can be hard being a teenager.

"I'm not saying that as any form of downplaying what he did or making excuses for him. I'm just saying that a lot of kids your age are handed a lot of social responsibility that you aren't equipped to handle yet...if that makes sense."

It still sounded like he was making an excuse, but I let him continue. I didn't know what I wanted to say. There was no way he'd defend Brandon.

"Sometimes, the results of the decisions people make aren't clear when they make them. I don't feel that what happened was Brandon's intention. He isn't a murderer and I'm sure he didn't *really* wish someone dead. Maybe the results of his decision got away from him this time. That's something he is going to have to face in many ways the rest of his life."

"But why does he get to live, and Jake doesn't? How is that fair?" I was getting worked up again.

He waited for my breathing to slow a little before answering. "As much of a cliché as it is, life doesn't work out that way. Life isn't fair."

I was getting frustrated, with all of this. I still didn't understand the answer to my main question, *Why?*

"Why would anyone post that video, though? You know you are going to screw up someone's life. Brandon knew, and he did it anyway. I don't get that."

"Sometimes, it's just about being able to. The power to influence people...

"Did I tell you that I got my EMT certification back in college? No? Well, I wasn't planning on working as one. I just had to take some extra health credits and it made sense to learn those skills just in case I was ever in a situation where I'd need them later.

"We sat in classes for six months learning about anatomy, first aid, CPR, and things like medications and ambulance operations. Not once did they teach us about real empathy. They taught some basic phrases we could say to emotional people to calm situations, but not the real substance behind them.

"Empathy is something that is incredibly hard to learn. A lot of it has to do with things like how you were raised, how you see yourself, and other factors, but it isn't something that can really be taught in a quick class.

"So, what happens is you get a lot of types of people becoming EMTs and doctors who have various levels of empathy for other people. Sometimes it means you have people who join those professions because they like the feeling they get being in power and being the hero; I think it's called the superhero complex or something. Some people join because of genuine concern for their fellow man and just want to help. Some go down that route because they just love the science or the medicine.

"That's an overgeneralization and there are a lot of other types, but the point was that there is a lot of variety in terms of the motivations and methods people have for doing what they do, but they're expected to operate in the same environment and have the same results.

"What I found to be the case is that these motivations directly impacted how they interacted with patients. The superheroes became domineering, the empathetic became too emotionally connected, which makes it difficult to make the hard decisions and cope with the loss of a patient, and the emotional detachment from the purely scientific or medical ones would make patients feel like a piece of meat on a lab table, like this," he said, tapping the palm of his hand down on the table we were sitting at.

"I don't for a second think that any of these people would ever wish harm or intend to cause emotional distress on someone else, but in their own ways, they unintentionally can. Every patient is different, and every situation is different.

"Some people need to divorce themselves from those emotions and distance themselves from their patients in order to think clearly, but it comes at a cost to the patient sometimes.

If you get in the habit of doing that for every call, you can turn into a bit of a robot.

"In that line of work, a significant amount of the people you meet are having the very worst or last day of their lives. They are looking up to you for help, help doing something they can't do on their own. Either for themselves or for a loved one. They are very vulnerable.

"In that position, you have a lot of responsibility. You, in part, become responsible for their emotional state.

"You have a choice. You can either embrace that and help them through it emotionally as best you can in addition to doing the medical service, or you can distance yourself and tell yourself it isn't your responsibility.

"Not that they are dismissing the patient's feelings so easily, it's just they might *need* the distance for their own sake and feel that it's more important they are able to function over their patient's emotional state, which I can understand.

"When you're getting your certification, you have to work in an emergency room for a day as well as an ambulance. They called them ride alongs. You put on your student uniform, which looks like the real deal, but with a big *Student* label on the patches. You have your pen in your shirt pocket and scissors in a special one on the outside of your cargo pants pocket. You have your stethoscope slung around your neck like a good hospital drama on TV. And you march up ready to go.

"When I was working in the ER, it was about halfway through the day, and all morning it had been a lot of fun. Small injuries. I got to get hands-on for a lot of things I wouldn't have outside those doors. It felt good and I can still remember the excitement I felt. To this day, I can't tell you what their faces looked like, or even their names. I was just so interested in the magnitude of what I was doing.

"Just after I got back from lunch, we received word that there was an ambulance about five minutes out that had a child who was hurt pretty badly. I felt the adrenaline pumping

111

and excitement building. It was a weird feeling because, if you can't tell by my profession, I love kids. I never want to cause or witness them in pain. But for some reason, I felt a weird excitement.

"I stood back and watched the ambulance arrive to give the doctors and nurses room to move, but I was still in the room. I walked with one of the nurses to escort the parents out of the ER and into the family room and helped settle them in. The whole time they were begging to see their child and telling us we needed to save her and help her and to not let her die.

"I was twenty-one years old at the time and didn't know what it was like to be a parent or be in that kind of position, so I felt really uncomfortable and tried to leave the room as fast as I could. I wanted to get away from the parents and go watch what was happening in the ER. They were looking at me the same way they were looking at the nurse who was with me. Like I had the power to decide whether their child would live or die.

"The nurse was able to help them settle, so we were able to go back to the ER, but I don't even remember how she did it. I was that detached.

"We went back to the ER just in time to witness the little girl, maybe three years old, struggle extensively, then fade away. The doctors tried everything they could, and the entire room was organized chaos as everyone did their absolute best in a terrible situation. They were professionals.

"I watched that child die, and I watched a little part of everyone in that room die as well. When they declared time of death, the lead doctor stood over her from up near her left shoulder, looking down to her still body, defeated. One of the nurses threw out her nitrile gloves and slowly washed her hands in the sink from what appeared to be muscle memory before sitting in the corner of the room and burying her head in her hands. And another left the room without saying a word."

Mr. Hunter paused for a minute. I could see in his face that this was very difficult to talk about.

"When I stepped outside, I saw the nurse who left before me walk toward another room where a patient was waiting. She paused outside the door for a second, took a deep breath, and lifted her head up and shoulders back, then walked into the room. She greeted them kindly and asked about their problem with a smile and a friendly tone.

"I don't know how she did it. I don't know how she turned it on and off like that, but she did it for the patients she was about to treat. She knew that they were having a hard day, and they came to this hospital, and indirectly to her, in order to seek support. She took that responsibility seriously. If she were to walk in there carrying the baggage of what had happened just twenty feet away and just moments before, it would have put a lot of unnecessary stress on her next patients.

"The family room in the ER had a glass window on one of the sides, which was visible from the nurses' station. I stood over there when the doctor left the little girl to be cleaned up and to notify the parents.

"He removed his gown, washed his hands, and reviewed some more paperwork before walking toward the room. I saw him do the same thing that the other nurse did. He paused, took a deep breath, pulled his shoulders back and head up, and walked in.

"I couldn't hear what he said through the privacy soundproofing, but I could see in his face that he had a deep sadness. He gestured to the chairs in the room, but the parents refused. As he spoke, probably explaining what had happened to her and the medical steps he'd taken to try and save her, the mother of the girl started to shrink. She was getting lower and lower as her husband, standing behind her, tried to hold her up with both hands on her upper arms.

"When the doctor stopped talking, she sank. She fell to the floor to her knees, arms loose at the shoulder and just hanging to the floor. The husband wasn't able to hold her up because he was in shock as well. He just stood there.

"At that point, the doctor could have walked out. Medically speaking, there was nothing in that room that would have helped his patient, the child. He notified them of what had happened, so he had technically done his job. But he stayed.

"He got down onto his knees and put his right hand on her shoulder and kept talking to her. Eventually, she was able to look up at him, and he was able to help her move to a nearby couch in the room. The husband joined her a second later. Only once they were settled did he leave the room."

Mr. Hunter was sitting there with his hands together in front of him on top of the table, and he was fidgeting with his nails and fingers as he spoke. This was weighing on him heavily.

"Later that day, I was able to pull the doctor aside to ask him about how he was able to do that, and if other doctors took that time to comfort people. He said that they teach a lot of that in med school and in residency but acknowledged that a lot of doctors don't do it well.

"What he told me has stuck with me heavily the rest of my life. He said he didn't know if this was the real name for it, or what it was called, but he called it empathic responsibility. He said that their emotional state was, in a way, dependent on what he said and how he behaved. He was in the position to either contribute to an already great pain by being distant and dismissive of their feelings and emotions, or he could do whatever he could to help them navigate those feelings in order to lessen the blow.

"He said that he knew it was a very minor positive impact given the severity of the situation, but he was making the conscious decision to not contribute to the negative, no matter how hard it was for him personally. Because, at the end of the day, he knew he was going to be able to go home to his family, and they wouldn't. He could take some pain, to help them process theirs."

He paused for a minute and took a sip from his coffee mug. I could tell that he needed the caffeine. He was exhausted, probably from a lack of sleep and the emotional weight of losing a student and player.

"Now, the reason I told you all of that is because of that concept of empathic responsibility," he said with strong emphasis. "He knew he had the power to inflict greater emotional pain on top of what was already there or help reduce it. He knew his actions would have an impact, so he felt the responsibility to be empathetic and compassionate.

"Now, I don't know if Brandon is homophobic. I don't know why he did what he did. But if you don't have that understanding of empathic responsibility, you become inherently self-centered in your decisions. Almost everyone is guilty of this from time to time. Maybe he saw a benefit to himself by posting that video that extended beyond the feeling of being responsible for Jake's emotional state. I don't know. But at your age, it's a tough ability to have. Especially in the moment when emotions and hormones are high, which is unfortunately the most important time for it to be used."

He pushed his body more upright in the chair with his hands on the corner of the table and took a deep breath, which changed the tone of his voice.

"Like I said yesterday, we don't know what was going through either Jake's or Brandon's minds, and we don't know why they did what they did. Only they do, and even then only to a certain degree. And I don't want you to take what I said as my interpretation of Brandon specifically. I haven't seen him or spoken to him since practice two days ago.

"The reason I said all of this is that I hope one day that kids your age better understand the impact that their actions can have on each other emotionally, can act responsibly in order to cause the least harm and relieve it whenever they can.

"With social media, and all the other communication methods you all have, it's even more important now. I'm afraid that the lessons needed to learn this are still taking too long and at too great a cost.

"I had to witness a three-year-old die before my eyes to learn it, and I was nineteen years old, not fourteen like you guys. I hope no one else needs to have such a strong-handed teacher. In some ways, this situation may have been that strong for some. But I just feel that it's a problem we will all have to face for a while."

He paused again, to let that sink in.

"You're a good kid. A great kid. I know from your reaction that you genuinely care about people. That is an amazing quality, but it will also cause a lot of pain in your life. The next while will not be easy for you. But you are asking the right questions and you are demonstrating that you are learning. Who knows, maybe next time something like this comes around, you can help be one of the ones who stops it before it goes this wrong."

I had been sitting there silently while he spoke, looking down at the table. It felt weird getting a compliment at a time like this. I did not feel like I deserved it.

"But I didn't prevent it. It happened," I said, frustrated.

"You weren't alone. A lot of us feel a burden… as we should," he said kindly. "I saw them arguing before practice and missed the opportunity to get more information behind it. If I'd have known, maybe I could have stopped it."

He paused. Clearly this was bothering him deeply.

"But one thing to think about too is that the video was probably just the tipping point. Since the family told people what happened, we can talk about it, but what happened to Jake was likely the result of something much deeper than one incident. Maybe if we prevented the incident from happening, things would be different. But what happened was probably influenced by a lot of factors over a long period of time. It was just a very strong one that tipped the scales.

"Again, in no way am I saying that posting the video wasn't terrible. It was. But what I'm trying to say, horribly as it turns out, is that suicide is a step someone takes based on a lot of complex emotions and mental states. It's rarely based on one incident without the influence of others. We can sit here and try to work it all out, but unfortunately the person who could help us understand what contributed to it is no longer with us.

"What we *can* do is take what happened and learn from it so we can do our best to help people in the future. We can use *empathic responsibility* to choose to help others when we have the power to influence them, rather than satisfy some of our own temporary emotional needs.

"With empathy comes emotional intelligence... or is it the other way around? I don't know, I'm tired. But we learn to read other people's emotions better and identify when they need help before it's too late. Now, I'll get in a lot of trouble from the school for saying all of this, but it's the truth that I'm going to have to accept for myself.... A lot of people missed the signs for Jake, and we may have missed some early bullying signs from Brandon. I'm really going to get in trouble for saying that.

"But I want you to know that you are not alone in your feelings and frustrations. This is on a lot of people."

I didn't know what to say, so I just nodded. This was a lot to digest.

"So, what happens now?" I asked.

He paused for a long time, thinking about this question.

"Well, I'm going to nerd out here, but try to stay with me. I look to science," he said with a small laugh. "Something happened that was horrible. But if we treat life like a science experiment, when something goes wrong, we carefully analyze as many of the facts as we can. Learn what contributed to the situation and theorize what needs to change in order for it to be successful next time. Redo the math, change the conditions, who knows. But we take what happened and we learn so that next time the results are different.

"Engineering has a process aptly called 'design, test, build.' If you design a plane, you come up with a wing design, you test it every which way you can, and if it works, you build it. When you have that wing design, you bend it until it breaks, you expose it to extreme heat and extreme cold, you put it in a wind tunnel to test how air flows over and under it, and how that air behaves when they converge afterwards.... Things will work, and things won't, so you go back to your design to fix the things that didn't and try again.

"With what is happening around us right now, it's clear that we are still in the testing phase, and we need to keep readjusting the design. The air is too turbulent, we may be using the wrong materials that crack under extreme temperatures, who knows. But at the end of the day, we aren't ready to build.

"We may never get there, but we will keep trying. Who knows, maybe they will discover some new material that can stand the heat, or some new principle of aerodynamics that will change how we look at the airflow. But we will never learn if we stop testing and accept the design we have now."

We sat there in silence for a few minutes. There was something about the way he spoke that just made sense to me. I was still digesting what he said, but I felt like I could understand where he was coming from.

"What did you do yesterday when you got home after our talk in the gym?" he asked, redirecting the conversation.

"I have a puppy that I took for a walk and played around with a bit. But nothing else really... I just needed to clear my head."

"You have a puppy? That's fantastic. Dogs are the best to help through times like this... What's its name? Is it a boy or girl?"

"It's a boy. I don't have a name yet. I'm still trying to figure it out."

He sat there for a minute. "Names are hard," he said, thinking intently.

"Since you're a space nerd, like I am, have you thought about something themed along those lines?" he asked.

"A little, but it's hard to find something that isn't used to death. NASA, Astro, Astra for a girl... it's all used too much... I don't know."

"Have you thought about going down the Greek route? The names of the constellations can be a little boring, but the stories behind how their names came to be can be really interesting and you might find a name you like with some meaning. I loved reading about it in college."

I had a feeling he was going to geek out more, but it was comforting to hear him talk for some reason.

"Do you know the story behind the Canis Major and Canis Minor constellations?"

I shook my head.

"They actually come from the story about a hunting dog and a fox. The dog was named Laelaps and was originally a gift to Europa from Zeus, but he had a very rough history around its owners. Definitely look up the whole story. I would bet you will see a lot of similarities with the situation we have now... But basically, Laelaps was the perfect hunting dog that always caught its prey and was extremely loyal to its owners. The fox, I forget its name, but it was the perfect fox; no one could catch it. So, there was this paradox of the fox that can't be caught with the dog that always catches its prey.

"The hunt was never going to end, so Zeus turned them both into stone, and threw them into the stars as the Canis Major constellation for Laelaps, and Canis Minor for the fox. Forever in the chase."

Just then, the bell rang, signaling the end of lunch.

He started to stand up from his stool and grabbed his lunch bag.

"I hope I helped, Tyler. But just in case you haven't yet, please go have a quick chat with Dr. Becker. She is very good. I had a long talk with her yesterday and I really hope you will too."

"I know, I will. I just don't know what to talk about yet," I said as I gathered my trash and packed up what remained of my lunch.

"You don't have to know what to say when you get there. Just go. I promise it will help."

Part 2

11

I was always early.

When I was early, I could sit down, get something to drink, and just gather myself before the other person got there. Walking in second was always awkward. I'd be spotted across the restaurant or cafe, I'd do the uncomfortable chin up nod to acknowledge we'd seen each other, then make the long, quiet walk over to the table, trying not to make so much eye contact I tripped on someone else's chair on the way over.

I was about ten minutes early this time, which gave me plenty of time to get seated and try to strategize. There was nothing really to strategize, but thinking about the impending scenarios gave me something to focus on and feel like I had a game plan.

They never went as planned, but I still tried.

Faces were hard for me. After all these first dates, more than I was willing to admit, I struggled to differentiate girls in public. Their faces started to turn into a homogenous figure of a girl who matched my normal type.

This felt very shallow and like I wasn't trying hard.

I was trying. I swear.

Every girl was unique, and there was something about each and every one I went on a date with that drew me toward them. But it was often not a physical thing, so it was difficult to differentiate by mental picture.

Some worked for a cool company or had a job that I was interested in hearing more about. Some had upbringings similar to mine, so I thought it was a good basis for communication. Some just had a lot of interest in me, which, I'll be honest, I liked. Not a lot of people showed a ton of interest these past few years, so it felt good.

No, that last one is *not* a good basis for a new relationship, but I was tired. I had gone on too many of these and was slowly losing energy.

Sometimes, you know it's not enough for a good start, but you go anyway. I would tell myself, *Maybe there is something I didn't see that I'll like. Or I've never been successful at this game, so what do I know about picking criteria?*

So, there I was.

This particular date didn't have much beyond a general curiosity around her job, but maybe that was enough.

Since I was focusing on that, I needed to try to focus harder on her face. There was nothing worse than not recognizing your date.

I pulled out my phone and opened up the app we'd met on, casually scrolling through her pictures one at a time in an effort to identify and memorize features that I felt were unique enough for me to spot in a public setting.

This was *way* more difficult than you'd expect.

I know it was over-generalizing to say all girls looked alike, but it was true when it came to online dating.

There seemed to be a formula they all wanted to match. Like, *this worked for one of my friends, so I'll try to match it in the hopes I have the same luck.*

First picture they had was with one or two friends who looked very similar. Same style hair, similar clothing since it was often at a winery or a bar, which typically had a certain standard attire, and people with similar styles tended to gravitate toward each other in friendships.

One friend was usually much more attractive than the other, which was intentional since it was essentially bait to get the quick swipe "yes" at the first sight of her, then you'd find out later it wasn't her and you got mildly catfished.

I never understood that. "Let's start this relationship off with duping each other…"

And if you did swipe based on that one pic, it didn't matter if she was the attractive one or not. You were admitting you were only basing your decision on looks, which was a trait all girls loved to openly hate on.

So, why tailor your profile to those types of guys? Why deliberately set yourself up for failure?

Whatever.

The second picture was usually one from another app that had photo filters. You know the ones. The ones that softened or blurred the image, overlaid fake freckles, enlarged cartoon or anime eyes, and some form of rodent ears or cartoon tiara on the top of the head.

You know, the ones that distorted what you actually looked like and made you match *every single other girl* who had used that photo filter.

OMG, this makes me look so cute, they must have thought…

I'm sorry, but you just looked like every other girl who used that filter.

So, I was now two pictures down into the profile and struggling to identify any majorly unique features. And I needed a majorly unique one since they often overdid the makeup on date one, hiding freckles, skin tones, using new hairstyles or getting it cut since the pictures were taken, or even having different eye color thanks to colored contact lenses.

On to number three…

Damnit! It was just another generic one from a distance aimed at her back in some outdoor setting. Hiking on the top of a hill, near a waterfall, at a beach… It didn't matter, they were all the same. It was just a picture to showcase body shape. But since it was always a pose they weren't going to make in the restaurant, and there was nothing else in the picture to get an accurate height guess, it didn't matter.

(FYI, it was true. Everyone lied about height, so you couldn't trust the numbers in the bio.)

I couldn't go up to every girl of a similar shape and ask, "Can you go stand fifteen feet away from me, look at the far wall, and raise both your arms at about forty-five degrees above your head and spread your feet two to two and a half feet apart from each other like you're having a spiritual moment embracing the rising sun?"

That would be creepy as fuck.

Yes, I could ask what her name was before that, but that would be awkward too. "Hey, are you Amy?" always got me "What? You don't recognize me from my pictures? You must have not been trying hard enough..." or something similar.

If... *if...* they had a fourth picture, it was usually something helpful. But it was rarer than you'd think.

Oh, thank god... she had one.

Okay, light cheek dimples, discernible nose shape... probably enough to go off of.

After quickly rereading the back-and-forth texts from the past two days as a conversation refresher, I put my phone down on the table in front of me and tried to relax before she got there.

I deliberately aimed my chair toward the front door of the coffee shop to be able to spot her arrival early enough to not be snuck up on. I wasn't comfortable though; I was constantly looking up every few seconds to see if she was there, which prevented me from relaxing.

After a few more minutes, I saw someone who I felt matched what I thought I identified in that fourth picture. I smiled faintly toward her, something not too strong just in case it wasn't her, as I didn't want a stranger to feel uncomfortable.

Guessing incorrectly typically resulted in very suspicious backward glances and "Why is that bearded creep smiling at me?" It was a great way to build confidence right before meeting someone else for a first date...

Thankfully, my smile was returned with the standard nod before she walked in my direction.

Standing up from my chair as she approached, I said, "Hi, Amy. How's it going?"

"Good!" she said, as we gave each other an awkward and light hug before she sat down across from me at the small table.

"Can I get you a drink or anything?"

"Oh, no thanks. I don't drink coffee."

Okay…. then why had she agreed to meet at a coffee shop?

"Um, okay, want any tea or anything?" ⸢SEP⸣

"No, I'm good. Thanks."

I had already gotten a hot mocha with an extra espresso shot to prevent me from yawning on the date. It was a real risk when I was tired from overthinking about it all.

So, this was already awkward right off the bat.

What do I do? Do I keep drinking my drink even though she doesn't have one? Or do I just let it sit so we are the same? I never knew what to do in these situations.

Whatever, just talk and don't look weird.

"Okay, sounds good. Thanks for meeting up. I was pretty excited to meet up with you after finding out you're an engineer. I really wanted to be one. Do you like it?"

"Yeah, it's fine."

I sat there, waiting for an expansion on the answer that I could grab on to to ask a follow-up question and keep the conversation going.

It didn't come.

"How did you pick medical devices?" I asked, hoping she'd expand.

"My dad is a doctor, so it just made sense," she said matter-of-factly.

"Cool, what kind of medical devices? I got my EMT certification in college, so it's cool to learn about the new things people are making."

"Insulin pumps."

These two- to three-word answers were killing me.

"That's cool. Any particular reason you got into that area, any diabetic family or friends?"

"Nope."

Ugh….

Maybe a joke would open this up a bit.

"So, I probably shouldn't have gotten this sugar-filled drink then. Might be one of your customers someday."

I knew it was a stupid joke. Pumps were typically for type one diabetes. Adult onset is type two and rarely needs such a severe treatment device.

"We don't make them for type two," she said, a little judgmentally, surely questioning my EMT comment from before.

"I know, it was just a bad joke."

Well, this was off to a great start.

She scrunched her right cheek before lifting her head in an acknowledging nod. Not a laugh.

She looked down at her phone that hadn't buzzed or rung.

"Oh, shit. I'm sorry. I forgot I agreed to meet up with my friend and her husband right now. Can we reschedule? She's been asking for weeks to hang out."

She couldn't have been more obvious.

But it was okay. It was clear this was going nowhere.

"Yeah, of course. No worries," I said, knowing that there would be no rescheduling.

"Thanks! It was great meeting you. I'll text you," she said as she stood up and quickly pushed her chair back under the table.

"Sounds good. Have fun," I said, not bothering to stand up and give her a hug as she left.

She made her way out the front door she had just come in maybe five minutes before...

I just sat there and finished my cooling drink.

12

"**W**ell?" A familiar voice from behind surprised me. I was so focused on work that I forgot there were people around me.

"How did it go?"

Turning away from the disturbing number of spreadsheets on my computer screen, I was greeted by a smiling face with an inquisitive expression.

"Hey, Lauren... Not great. Lasted an awkward ten minutes. Pretty disappointed," I said.

Lauren's smile got instantly bigger as she tried to hold it in...

She ended up bursting it out far too loud for our crowded office... "*That's what she said!*"

I looked around at my cubicle neighbors to see everyone looking in my direction. This office was one of those stupid "open office" designs where no one had any privacy. So, with any real noise, everyone made uncomfortable eye contact.

Whoever thought this design was a good idea should never be allowed to design offices again. This was an introvert's worst nightmare. No privacy and a ton of distractions.

"Damnit. I can't set you up like that," I said, now with a light smile on my face.

"Yeah, you walked right into that one. So, what happened?" she asked before putting on a parental smug look on her face, looking down her nose at me. "What did you learn from the experience?"

She was two years younger than I was, so this frustrated the hell out of me.

I let out a fake chuckle and said, "I learned that online dating blows."

"See, that's your problem. You are in an age of infinite choices and opportunities. Live in the moment. Take in the field!" She was sarcastic as hell sometimes. It was one of her most endearing qualities.

"*You* might have all the choices and opportunities. It's different for guys," I said, a little more seriously, trying to ride her sarcastic comment to prove a point that had been bugging me for the last few years.

"What do you mean? Don't play victim now. It's not a trait girls look for in a man."

"That's exactly what I mean."

I shuffled in my chair, pulling my right foot up to tuck it under my left thigh.

"All the girls I see on these things have such an influx of messages that they essentially have so many options to choose from, they shop for very specific traits," I said, a little frustrated.

"Look. I did the math. I send about ten to fifteen messages a week to start conversations with new matches. Only about one or two get responses. That's an average of around ten percent return."

Lauren sat there, rolling her eyes.

"Don't do the math. You can't do that for these kinds of things," she said, shaking her head.

"I can't help it. Every guy I know says the same thing. So, that means girls are getting an excessive number of messages every week and can afford to cherry-pick the ones to respond to based on whatever criteria they want. Six feet tall, rich, thick hair... Whatever they want. Because, statistically, they have four or five who match that criteria in their inbox at any given time."

I was getting worked up a little. This system sucked.

"Women get to shop. Men get to gamble."

Lauren let out a laugh, giving us another wall of angry stares from the cubicles nearby.

"Sounds like the tables have finally turned! The women have the power!"

It was my turn to roll my eyes.

"Whatever."

She was still giggling a little.

"Don't whatever me. Whatever you're doing on these dates must be the problem. They seem to be spectacular. Spectacularly short, or end in spectacular flames."

"I'm sure there is something I'm doing wrong, but it's not like I can email them an online survey to fill out to get the details. I'm a little shit up a creek here in terms of feedback."

Lauren sat there for a second thinking hard before a huge, almost devious smile broke out on her face.

"I have an idea. Let's go on a date."

"What?" I said, doing a double take. "Really? No, you just want to see me fail hard. I'll wear a GoPro next time and you can watch from a distance."

"No. I'm serious. Let's go on a date. I want to see you in action. I want to see you pull your best moves."

"Come on. This won't work," I said, slightly embarrassed.

"You don't have a choice. You're taking me to dinner on Friday night."

Before I could even respond, she jumped up from the stool she was sitting on near my desk and walked away.

"See you Friday at seven thirty," she said over her shoulder as she strolled down the line of cubicles toward her desk.

Amazed and confused at what had just happened, all I could do was turn back to my desk and stare at the wall of spreadsheets again, barely able to focus.

But strangely, I was smiling…

Well, I was early again.

I knew this restaurant was crazy busy on Fridays and they didn't take reservations for only two people. So, I got there early to make sure we weren't going to be standing awkwardly in the doorway forcing conversation quietly so all the other people standing shoulder to shoulder couldn't hear us.

Lauren loved sushi.

I figured that if she was going to be judging me on this mock date, I had to try, or she'd never let me hear the end of it. This place was a bit of a drive out from the valley, but it was worth it. I'd heard it would be really good from a few friends and wanted to try it out anyway.

Going out there for a date was a real ask of someone I was meeting for the first time. Asking someone to drive through a small canyon for forty-five minutes to meet someone they didn't know had a bit of a serial killer vibe. And I didn't like going to these kinds of places alone.

So, Lauren got good sushi, I got to try out a new restaurant, and I got bonus points for picking somewhere decent.

Win, win, win.

I was sitting pretty comfortably with a glass of Sapporo when Lauren got there and sat down across from me at the tiny table.

She was wearing a black dress without sleeves that was tight to her slender figure and caught me off guard.

She was beautiful.

I must have not hidden it well, because as soon as she sat down and hung her purse on the hook under the table, she looked at me with a smile and said, "You can stop staring at me now."

"What? Oh, sorry. Hey."

"Wow, awkward from the start. I like where this is going," she said, the smile getting bigger with every second.

"You don't exactly wear things like that at work. It surprised me a little," I said with a tinge of shyness in my voice.

"That bad, huh? I mean, I know I'm slumming here with you, but geez."

"No! It's great. I like it," I said, trying to recover. I knew full well she was just messing with me and knew it was a positive comment, but she just needed to jab at me. It was her style.

"Relax. Your eyes told me what your words totally failed at."

I started to blush a little.

She must have noticed because she quickly put both her forearms on the table and joined her hands together, took a deep breath, and looked right at me before saying…

"I want wine, sushi, and your best moves."

"Well, you can definitely get the first two, but the third will be questionable," I said, right eyebrow raised sarcastically.

"Good. All I really wanted was a free meal," she said matter-of-factly.

"Perfect."

The waitress walked over once she saw Lauren get settled into her chair and got her drink order of the house white wine before scurrying off to return with the much-needed booze that was essential for this awkward date to function smoothly.

"Okay, let's do this," Lauren said, clearly super excited to see me flounder.

"This is weird! I don't know where to start. You already know me," I said, struggling to come up with what to say.

"I know Work Tyler, not Real Tyler. Tell me about Real Tyler."

"They are pretty similar… I don't know," I said, thinking hard about what I was supposed to say.

"Bullshit. There is much more than what I see at work. You're thinking too hard about this. Stop thinking so hard."

I laughed… "Do you know me at all?"

"Exactly. You overthink. Just relax and tell me what makes you tick. What are your deepest fears, your shallowest thoughts, your favorite holiday, your hated celebrity trend? Small talk, Tyler!"

"Those aren't small!"

"Okay, fine. Ask me a question," she said, leaning back a little in her chair.

"Um… How was the drive out here?" I asked, saying the first thing that came to mind.

"It was fine, not a lot of traffic. Okay, my turn now. What is your favorite sex position?"

I almost spit out the beer I had just taken a sip of.

"*What?* You can't lead with that!"

"Why not?" she asked, trying to hold back a huge smile and play it seriously. "Mine is cowgirl. And on a good ass day, maybe reverse cowgirl."

At that exact moment, the waitress walked up next to Lauren to slide the glass of white wine onto the table. She *clearly* heard what Lauren had just said out loud but was trying to be professional and hide the grin before speaking up.

"H—Hi there… Have we had a chance to take a look at the menu?"

We both laughed a little under our breath out of embarrassment.

"Yes," Lauren said. "We are going to share a couple rolls."

She pulled up the menu off the table to hold it in front of her and the waitress.

"We will get a spicy tuna roll, the Stargazer roll, and some edamame to start. Thanks."

The waitress quickly wrote down the order and nodded politely before running off, leaving the menus behind. Probably glad to avoid the awkwardness of our conversation.

"Ordering for me? Are we already at that point in our relationship?" I said curiously, with a smile. I was looking at the Stargazer roll anyway, but still. It was a basic California roll style inside but had salmon on top with some spicy mayo, my favorite. No idea why it had that name, but specialty sushi roll names never made sense to me.

"You're a sushi amateur, and I feel like I know what you'd like. Plus, if you had it your way, you'd get a roll to eat by yourself, and I'd get mine. Sushi is about sharing! Now you have no choice."

"Fine. I mean, you ordered what I wanted anyway. But still… I need to wear the pants in this relationship!" I said sarcastically.

"If you're lucky, no pants will be involved in this relationship," she said with a devious smile.

"Damn, I can't set you up like that."

"I'll set you up," she said quickly back.

"Oh, come on. That was weak. You could do better."

"Fine. Whatever," she said, looking down at her lap with a half-cracked smile as she adjusted the cloth napkin across her thighs.

"Back to this critical line of questioning. Tell me how you tick," she said, looking back at me as she leaned forward onto her elbows, hands under her chin, holding up her head.

"That's not a question, that's a command!" I said jokingly.

"Fine... tell me something... tell me something weird. I mean, I know you're weird. But tell me something that you think is weird about you," she said more seriously.

I laughed back. "You'll need to be more specific. I'm pretty weird."

"Okay, fine, let's see... Tell me about being an EMT. Girls love a guy who can save a life. What was the weirdest thing about being an EMT?"

"The weirdest? That is a very weird question," I said with a chuckle.

"Come on. Did you think I wouldn't be weird tonight? You don't know me at all. I need to ask the hard questions."

"Okay, okay... Let me think."

I sat there for a few seconds, running through all the answers I had. There were a lot of things that were weird, but I wasn't sure what I should share. What if something wasn't weird to her? I didn't want her to think I was crazy, and I didn't want her to feel weird for thinking something wasn't weird.

I was overthinking this.

"Awkward silences are always fun on dates. Keep it up," she said sarcastically.

"Sorry! Okay, I know something. You know I didn't work as an EMT, right? I just got the certification in college."

"I know. Overachiever. Go on," she said, twirling her right wrist in a circle with her index finger pointed to keep the conversation moving.

"Well, the weird thing is you never get to relax after you go through that training. You're always running through scenarios in your head, ready to pounce if something happens."

"That's not that weird," she said back, seemingly disappointed by my answer.

"For me it was," I said back quickly.

"Why?"

"In training, you are taught to go through a scenario start to finish. So, if you were showing up to an injury, you'd run through the arrival at the scene, the patient assessment, the treatment, and the transport.

"That seems normal."

"I know. But now imagine that in my head. I run through all the conversations I have in those scenarios. Asking all the questions to the patient about the accident, mocking up the radio calls in, and everything else. And I'd have to finish."

She looked ready to burst with that last sentence. I stopped talking and waited for it...

"Okay, let it out..." I said.

"That's what she said!" she burst out. "Sorry, I had to."

"Damnit, Lauren!" I said with a smile on my face. It was a serious conversation. I should have known she'd throw a wrench into it.

"I'm sorry! Go on. You had to finish.... That's what she said."

"Well, I do that everywhere now. Every restaurant I'm in, I run through a choking scenario. Every car ride, I go through a car accident scenario. Every plane I'm on, I run through a heart attack scenario. Everywhere, all the time..."

"Okay, that is weird," she said with a pretty serious look on her face. "I'm exhausted just thinking about that. But on the bright side, you must be prepared for everything. I want to be around you if I'm ever in a bad situation."

I laughed. "Probably. But let's not find out."

Just then, the waitress appeared with the food. The edamame was late, so it got there with the sushi. Or the sushi was early. I don't know. Either way, everything arrived, and we shuffled the drinks and soy sauce trays to fit it all on the tiny table.

Lauren poured some soy sauce in her tray before handing the small bottle to me.

"Okay, you have to try both of these rolls before we speak another word... In other words, I'm hungry and need a moment of silence to inhale."

"Deal." I said.

"Shut up and eat," she said with a smile as she reached across to pick a piece of the stargazer roll off the long ceramic plate and brought it to her small tray.

As she reached over, I got a close look at the tattoo she had on the inside of her wrist. It was a fish that was drawn with tiny cursive words around its perimeter instead of lines, repeating *per aspera ad astra ~ per aspera ad astra ~....* I had seen it before, but not this up close.

At this distance, I saw something I'd never seen before. Raised skin along the back end of the tail fin. Like a scar that never fully healed or flattened.

She must have seen me staring because she pulled her hand back slowly with the small piece of sushi in her chopstick grip and placed it gently on her plate, looking down at it while shuffling it around slowly, positioning it on the plate.

"You can ask about it. It's okay," she said, looking up at me with her chin down.

"Sorry, I didn't mean to stare at it that long. I'm weird. Ignore me," I said quickly back, offering to move on from the subject.

"No, it's okay. I want you to ask me. You shared a personal weird thing. It's my turn."

"Um... okay... What's the story with your tattoo?" Not wanting it to be too obvious and pointed, I added a casual, "I've always wanted one, but never knew what I would get. Wanted it to mean something."

"Yeah, I got this one when I was twenty-two."

She paused for a second.

"Ready for shit to get real?" she said with a little laugh.

"I mean, we're already talking about reverse cowgirl and obsessing about car accidents and heart attacks. Why not?"

"Ha... good point," she said, before taking another sip of her wine.

"Back in college, I had a really hard time fighting depression. It got really dark for a while and I thought it wouldn't end. I wasn't doing as well as I wanted to in school, didn't know what I wanted to do after I graduated, the debt was piling up, and my dating life was even worse than yours... if you could imagine that."

"Did you lead those dates with sex positions and commandeering the food order?"

Damnit, Tyler, don't joke. She's telling something serious.

She laughed a little, which helped me relax a bit.

"Believe it or not, I wasn't so smooth back then."

"You call this being smooth?" I laughed.

"I'm having fun," she said with a smile. "Feels pretty smooth."

I couldn't help smiling back.

"Well, back then I didn't really feel like I had a ton of options or that things were getting better. It was kind of a perfect storm of little things. Nothing really big and catastrophic, but just a buildup of a ton of smaller things that I didn't know how to handle properly. So... I ended up cutting my wrist in the bathtub one night."

"Jesus," I said, not sure what else to say.

She let out a forced chuckle. "I know, right? Heavy."

"How are you now?"

"I'm great. Thankfully I cut in the wrong direction and lived, obviously. Went to therapy for a while, was on some medication. Now I'm great."

"Good," I said, putting a small smile back on my face.

"So, feel better knowing you aren't the crazy one at this table?" She laughed out loud.

"I don't think you're crazy."

"I do, so maybe we both are a little. It's cool. We can be crazy together." She was softly smiling back now. Not out of embarrassment. But for real, I think.

"But yeah, the tattoo... Once things healed in my head for the most part, there was a local tattoo artist who was doing self-harm cover-up tattoos for free. He lost a brother to suicide, so he did this on his own to give back to people who want to move past things.

"So, I figured I'd do something that would make it slightly less prominent to avoid the judgment that comes along with that kind of scar but would also act as a small reminder for myself of what I'd done.

"I felt that I didn't want to try to pretend like it never happened. Acknowledging that it happened was a key part for me to move past it. So, I picked a fish as both a stupid reminder to 'just keep swimming' and some sort of a bathtub metaphor. Personification? I don't know the word I'm trying to say. But you know what I mean.

"And, the Latin means *through struggles, you can reach the stars.* So, it's just a corny reminder that it was just a momentary struggle, but that it will ultimately lead to something good if I keep trying."

I sat there thinking about all of that. I'd known Lauren for a while now but had no idea about this. I don't think she was trying to hide it, but it just never came up. And I clearly wasn't looking hard enough until today.

"You're silent. Did I break you?" she said, dipping her forehead toward me, looking up inquisitively.

"No, no. Just a lot to digest."

"I know," she said with a small laugh. "Want to bail on me like your other dates?"

"No! Absolutely not."

"Good," she said with a bigger smile now.

"Thank you for telling me all that. I bet it was hard."

"I'm good talking about it now. Just wanted to make sure I didn't scare you away."

"I'm still here... But I'll admit... this is the most intense mock date ever."

We both laughed.

We ordered another round of drinks and another roll to share over some less dramatic conversations before the check came.

"Would you like a to-go box?" the waitress asked as she dropped the check folio on the edge of the table. There were maybe two pieces of the last roll left on the plate, which was definitely not enough to take home.

I grabbed an edge of a single piece of salmon with my fingers and lifted it up and held it out to Lauren.

"Would you mind putting this in your purse for the ride home?"

She laughed. "It was good, but not that good."

I looked back to the waitress and said, "No thanks," before pulling out my credit card and handing the folio back to her.

Yes, I wiped my hand on the napkin first. I wasn't an animal.

After grabbing our things, we made our way out to our cars in the parking lot.

"So, how did I do? Don't be gentle, tell me the truth."

She tilted her head to the side and looked up, as if deep in thought.

"Well, I see a lot of room for improvement. So, to keep your ego in check, maybe a C+ or a B-."

"Ouch!"

"I know, sorry. But the good news is that I'm willing to help you out more. You clearly need it."

I pretended to look shocked at the score, but her not-so-subtle way of asking for another date got me excited.

"Good, I was hoping you'd offer."

We gave each other a hug before getting into our cars and making the drive back through the canyon.

Normally, I listened to calmer alt rock or some classics when I drove, but I was pretty excited this time. So, I threw on some rock and hip-hop to match my heartrate.

I had a lot of fun.

As the road exited the canyon into the valley, I pulled to a stop at the red light and noticed Lauren's car was behind me.

After a few seconds, my dash beeped at me and a text message appeared on the screen.

"I'm following you home. I need to grade your third-date moves to see where you go wrong."

Before I could respond, the traffic light turned green and I had to go.

We parked at my apartment building and started the walk over to the elevator.

"Are you serious? My place is a wreck," I said, blushing nervously. I hadn't cleaned my apartment or anything since I wasn't expecting a visitor.

"Oh, come on. You saying something is dirty is like saying there is a speck of sand somewhere in a football field."

"Okay, fine. Don't say I didn't warn you."

I put the key into the door and pushed it open before walking in quickly ahead of her to see if there was anything I needed to hide. Too many Legos, video game T-shirts, candy... You never knew what I had lying around that an adult shouldn't...

She rushed in behind me fast. "Don't you dare try to hide anything!"

"I'm not!" I lied.

"Bullshit."

I was in the living room now, just off the main entryway, and she walked up behind me and dropped her purse on the end table next to the couch.

When I turned to face her, she was already standing next to me, our bodies almost against each other.

"Let's see how you do with a first kiss," she said before reaching up with her hands to gently grab both sides of my head to tilt it down.

I leaned in with a small head tilt to the side, and after placing both hands on her sides just above her hips, I closed my eyes and made gentle contact with her lips. It was soft and light at first, then we readjusted for more contact while my right hand moved up from her hip to her back.

When our lips separated, our heads rested together, foreheads touching.

With a light lick of her lips, she said, "Not bad. Not bad. But I'll need to try again just to be sure."

She tilted her head back again and pulled my head down to hers for a long, deep kiss. As I pulled her a little closer, she slid her right hand down the side of my face and gently placed her palm on my chest.

After a few seconds, she pulled her head back, bit her lower lip, and stood still.

Then, with a firm push on my chest, she stepped back and smiled.

She quickly grabbed her purse from the table and adjusted her dress down a little since it had ridden up as my hand moved up the small of her back.

"I think I have enough material for today's test. I'll be sure to send you my notes before next time."

I laughed. "What? Really? You're leaving?"

"What did you expect? I'm not that kind of girl, Tyler," she said with a wink before walking quickly back up to me, reaching up, and grabbing one last kiss before scooting off to the front door.

Not knowing what to say, I just stood there, shocked at what was happening.

The door slammed behind her, and it was over.

I collapsed on the couch, not sure what had just happened that whole evening. That had become a real date really fast. But I was okay with it.

A few minutes later, my phone buzzed with a new text message.

Lauren: *A+*

13

It had been a year since I had been in the same car as Luke. With work and school taking us to different places, the inevitable distance started to creep into our relationship.

I hated it.

When he said he was coming out to celebrate my engagement to Lauren, it made an amazing situation that much better.

I found this tiny sushi place out near the coast that was by far the best I'd ever had. I was never a sushi snob; I wasn't that adventurous. But there was something they did with the basics that made you feel like it was special. No matter how many times I tried to control myself whenever Lauren and I went, I always felt like I was going to explode stumbling to the car, feeling ten pounds heavier and a hundred dollars lighter.

When Luke came out, it was no different. Over-inflated with rice, salmon, and unagi sauce, we jumped into his car and started the drive back to my place. Luke's car was an amazing upgrade from the crappy car he had back in high school. Canvas was replaced with leather, window cranks for air were replaced with an automated climate system with electric windows, and the whining busted transmission was replaced with the pure silence of an electric single-gear motor.

It was unbelievably comfortable.

After the few drinks I'd had at the restaurant, I could totally pass out in the passenger seat while Luke drove us home. But it had been a while since I had so much time alone with him and I didn't want to waste a second of it.

"I still can't believe you got someone to agree to marry you," Luke said with a huge smile plastered on his face.

"I tried paying some other women to do it, but apparently that's not socially acceptable anymore. Trading a goat for a wife is inappropriate these days for some odd reason. I guess I just got lucky that she was free."

"Does she know you won't be a millionaire? Would be a shame for her to put some years in with you, only to have the money-grabbing divorce be unsatisfying. She was probably so excited when you didn't ask for a prenup. Probably banking on walking away with some serious cash," he joked back.

I looked over to my left in his direction with a serious look on my face. "Who says this isn't me trying to get the payout from her millions? I'm planning on working the system to be that trophy husband with a sugar momma."

It was pitch-black outside the car. I could only see the outline of Luke's face in the light glow from the dashboard lights. There was the consistent slow flash of light illuminating his whole face every few seconds as we passed under the street lamps lining the mountain road between the coast and the valley.

His laugh at what I said seemed accented by the lack of proper lighting. I could see the outline of his chest rise and fall and his neck muscles flexing with each laugh. It was perfectly visible through the casted shadows on his shirt as we passed under each streetlight.

He turned his head in my direction and said with a smile, "You're too ugly to be a trophy husband."

I let out a hard laugh at the same time as he did, the light from behind him giving his whole head a soft white glow down to his shoulders. The aura glow around him seemed to get brighter as he laughed, like the angel on someone's shoulder whispering into their ear. I wondered where the devil would be...

The light behind him got blinding quickly before I realized what it really was....

Like a bad movie, time stopped.

I could see Luke smiling, eyes facing forward now, ignorant to what was just outside his driver-side door.

For a split second, it went dark. The headlights from the other car ducked low, under Luke's window frame as the car smashed into his door.

It was the loudest noise I'd ever heard in my life.

Glass from his window shattered and flew outwards toward the other car, only to hit the other car's windshield and bounce back toward us. Glass flew across his face in my direction as the momentum from the other car transferred everything it had into ours. My head whipped to my left as the car was shoved, smashing it into the deployed side airbag as the car rolled onto its right side.

As the car slid along the asphalt, the glass from my window was now shattered, sending shards ricocheting off the asphalt next to my shoulder and into my face and chest. I had just enough time to bring my left forearm in front of my eyes to protect them from the razor-sharp pieces. My whole body weight was on my right arm, pinning it between my side and the car door.

After what seemed like forever, the car slowed down and slid to a stop, still on its side.

I was hyperventilating and trying to understand what had just happened.

"Lu—Luke... Are you okay?"

Silence.

"Luke! Can you hear me?" I yelled.

A groaning sound came from the air above my left shoulder.

"Don't move, Luke. Don't move," I said, barely able to speak, having lost my breath when the car pushed me onto my side hard. My EMT training was trying to take over, but I was struggling to breathe, preventing me from thinking straight.

Propping my body up a little on the deflated airbag with my right arm, I was able to reach down and unbuckle my seat belt with my left. Thankfully the passenger-side dashboard held its shape and I was able to free my legs and bring them under me with a lot of stumbling effort.

Now that my feet were on the ground, shoes crunching glass underneath them like dried-out seashells on rocks, I was able to slowly stand up sideways in the front cab of the car after pushing Luke's deflating steering wheel airbag out of the way.

Luke was covered in blood.

It was really dark, but I could still see it.

His head was cocked to his right, hanging down toward the floor. Blood was dripping from a hidden wound on the top of his head. I couldn't see the cut through the blood-soaked hair, barely illuminated by a distant streetlamp, but it was definitely there.

"Luke, don't move. I'm going to check you, but I don't want you to try to move anything."

Now facing him, I placed my left hand under his head to take the weight off his neck. If he had a spinal injury, I didn't want to raise his head straight with his body again. A bone fragment could sever his spinal cord if he was moved too much. I needed to hold it in place right where it was.

I could feel his warm blood on my hand, then my forearm as it oozed down my wrist.

What next? What next? What next?

I knew that I knew what to do next, but I couldn't breathe right, and it was making me dizzy and my head cloudy.

I needed to help Luke.

He needs me.

Take a deep breath and assess the situation.

I took a deep breath and felt a sharp stab in my right side, causing me to yell out as my body spasmed from the pain.

Shit. Shit. Okay.

I'm standing in a car that flipped on its side. The driver is barely conscious with a possible spinal injury. What now... What now?

Assess the patient.

"Don't move your head, Luke, at all. I'm going to check you for injuries, okay? Don't nod or shake your head. I need you to answer me with words only."

I glanced to the right of his face, down to his chest. His body was being held back into the bucket seat mostly by the locked-tight seat belt. Most of his weight was resting on the right side of the bucket seat and his waist and legs were resting along the car's center console. He was mostly stable, as long as the seat belt held.

"Can you tell me what hurts? Do you feel anything broken?" I asked, begging him to answer me.

Silence.

After a second or two, all I could hear was his breathing and a light mumble. The mumble was so quiet I couldn't make out any of the words.

"Okay, Okay, Okay," I said out loud, trying to calm myself down. My heart was pounding, and I could feel my hands starting to shake from the adrenaline.

I needed to keep the hand holding Luke's head steady. I couldn't risk moving him.

I made my right hand into a fist and squeezed it tight, then flexed all my fingers straight out a few times in the hopes that would help me calm the shaking. It seemed to work for a few seconds, so I took the small window to put two fingers on Luke's neck to feel his pulse.

146

Normally, I should have felt a strong and regular upward thump as the blood got forced through his carotid artery and into his brain.

That wasn't what I felt.

All I could feel were a few light bumps, and they were too far apart from each other for me to feel good.

Fuck.

Fuck.

Fuck.

"Luke! Stay awake, okay?"

The light above me disappeared, momentarily removing Luke from my view. I could only feel the blood slowly dripping down my hand, and the slow pulse in my right index and middle fingers....

Someone climbed onto the car to look down into the crushed and glass-ridden space Luke and I were in. I looked up to stare at a silhouette of someone's head and shoulders. With the only light behind him, I wasn't able to see his face.

"Are you guys okay?" he said fast with a breathy voice.

"Luke's fading. Call 911 right now! Tell them code three! Code three! One red, one green."

Code three meant shit was *not* okay.

He looked over his shoulder and yelled to someone I couldn't see.

"There are two in here! One seems okay, but the other isn't! He said to say..."

After a second of silence, he looked back down to me.

"Code three! It means get the fuck here. Now."

"Code three! Tell them code three!"

He looked back down to me. "They're on their way. We called as soon as we saw the accident. What can I do? What do you need me to do?"

"Are you able to climb into the back seat? I need help holding his head," I said, silently begging for him to say yes.

"Look away for a second. I need to kick out some glass. The doors are smashed, and I can't open them."

I put my right hand over Luke's eyes, even though they were already closed. And looked way.

With a few light kicks, he removed the remaining glass around the edges. Glass fell down to the ground, hitting pavement like rain. Thankfully, he seemed relatively young and was able to lower himself carefully into the back seat of the car.

"Please, Luke. Please stay awake."

He was now standing behind the front seats and looking at me around Luke's headrest with his back toward the roof of the car.

"I need you to hold his head and neck right where it is. Don't move it an inch. Can you put your hand on mine so I can slide it out for you to take over?"

He grabbed a loose T-shirt that Luke had on the back seat and wrapped it around his left hand before replacing mine with his. There wasn't a lot of blood on the left side of Luke's face, so he placed his uncovered right hand on Luke's left ear.

"Okay, I got him," he said, surprisingly calm.

I slowly slid my hand out from between his and Luke's right ear, careful to not move his head at all.

"Okay. Okay. Okay," I muttered to myself while I glanced up and down from Luke's waist to his head.

He was wearing a buttoned-up shirt, so it was easy to rip it open, exposing his chest and abdomen.

I leaned in to put my ear near his face to listen to his breathing. Air was moving, but it wasn't nearly as much as he needed to stay awake. I needed to keep an eye on that.

It was too dark to see much, so I put my hands on his chest by his throat and lightly pressed into him while moving them down his chest and stomach and around his sides to his back. I needed to feel if he had any more bleeding or major breaks or bulges under the pressure from my hands.

148

The left side of his body didn't feel right. Like there was too much of a gap between his ribs. Luke moaned a little when I touched them, so I knew something was wrong.

What do I do? I don't know how to fix this.

They didn't teach me how to fucking fix this shit!

Okay. Okay. Okay.

Breathe.

"FUCK!"

I yelled again, forgetting that I couldn't take deep breaths without being stabbed in the side. The guy holding Luke's head shook, startled from the outburst.

"What happened? Are you okay?" he asked, fear now overtaking his prior calm tone.

"Yeah." I paused, trying to breathe lightly through my nose. "My ribs just hurt... Try to hold still... Don't move his head...."

"Luke, you're hurt pretty bad, but help is already on its way, okay? I'm not going anywhere. I'm staying right here with you."

I tried to sound strong and supportive. I didn't even know if he could hear me. But what I'm sure came out was straight fear and panic.

I didn't know what was going to happen. I didn't want to think about what was going to happen. I just wanted this to never have happened. *What the fuck happened? Where is the other car? Where is the driver?*

I could feel my breathing get faster and my pulse race. *Where is the fucker who did this?*

Stay calm.

Stay calm.

Focus. What do I do? What am I supposed to do?

Stop the bleeding.

But I can't find it. It's too dark.

How do I stop something I can barely see?

I put my two fingers back on Luke's neck and felt for his pulse. It was still there, but it was getting weaker. I couldn't find any other serious bleeds, so I didn't think it was from a loss of blood. Unless it was internal or behind him where I couldn't reach... I put my other hand on his chest to feel for his chest to rise and fall with his breathing.

It was unbearably slow. I could feel it move, but its slow rate was making mine race. I was really worried.

This is NOT good. This is NOT good.

I got my EMT certification in college because I wanted to be prepared for stuff like this, like Mr. Hunter... I wasn't prepared.

After another minute of holding my hands on him, I was struggling to focus. I was repeatedly losing counts of breaths and heartbeats. My head kept clearing of any coherent thought process and flashing to nothing. Then I would flash back to reality as if waking up from a bad dream to a worse situation. I don't know how much time went by while I tried to keep monitoring Luke, but it felt like forever. Like when you were on the verge of falling asleep at night and couldn't tell how long your eyes had been half-open. Not awake enough to process time, not asleep enough to close your eyes.

Gradually, red and blue lights started to show onto the car's interior. I winced at the red because it made me instantly feel like everything was covered in Luke's blood. But the fast strobe interruption of blue and white light helped me realize it was just my head playing tricks.

I heard the sirens slowly increase in volume until they did their last flutter before falling silent. I could hear boots and engines nearby but couldn't see anything.

A few seconds later, a helmeted head appeared in the driver-side window, just like before. Except this time the flashing lights were illuminating his face brightly enough for me to squint.

"Everyone please stand as still as you can. I'm with the San Mateo County Fire Department. You, in the front, what's your name? Can you tell me what's happening?"

His face was now super illuminated, as floodlights from behind and to his sides were turned on and pointed toward us with blinding intensity.

"The car flipped after we got hit. My brother has a possible neck injury. We've been taking spinal precautions this whole time. And he has deformities on his left side and a head bleed."

"Are you in EMS?" he asked, not expecting that kind of answer.

"I was in college, but it was a long time ago," I said, hoping he understood I needed help.

"How's his breathing and pulse?" he asked calmly.

"Weak and slow. Really weak. Both of them."

"Okay, you're doing great," he said before turning his head to the side to speak with someone out of view. "There are three in here, two appear to be green, one red. Get the wedges underneath and the windshield off. We're going to have to get in through the roof.

"What are your names?" he said, looking at me and the man helping me from the back seat.

"Tyler... and this is Luke," I said, gesturing with my head. I couldn't will myself to take my hands off of Luke.

"Greg," the man in the back seat said. "I wasn't in the crash. I climbed in to hold his head. I'm not injured, but I think he is." He gestured with his head in my direction.

"Okay, thanks, Greg. My name is Ethan. Tyler, do you have any pain anywhere? How is your neck? Did you get any whiplash?" he asked, checking to see if I had a potential neck injury.

"My neck feels okay, but my right side hurts when I breathe too deeply. I think I broke a rib when I hit the side of the car."

"Okay, try to breathe slowly but deeply through your nose, and try not to move your head too much." His tone started to seem more scripted now. "I'll be here the whole time. I'm going to walk you through what's about to happen.

151

Ask me any questions you have, and I'll do my best to answer them for you."

I was beginning to feel better, knowing someone else was in charge. Someone who knew how to help Luke.

"We are going to have to cut off these top doors and remove the roof of the car. Normally, my guys would be the ones in your position holding Luke, but there isn't enough wiggle room for them to slide down and take over for you just yet, Greg. It would put too much risk of movement on Luke's neck. You're doing a great job holding him still like you are. I'll need you to keep doing that for just a bit longer."

Behind me, I could hear a fireman poking a crowbar into a hole at the edge of the windshield.

"Tyler, can you please cover Luke's eyes and turn *your* head toward the back of the vehicle? We are going to take the windshield off, and I don't want any glass to get into your eyes."

I turned my head after covering Luke's eyes, and could hear them peel the laminated windshield out from its sealed perimeter, and heard it crash to the floor as they threw it to the side.

"Tyler, there is a paramedic standing behind you, and I want him to be able to get a good look at Luke."

As he said that, I felt a steady hand rest on my right shoulder. The sound of flexing and stretching rubber gloves was audible next to my ear.

A calm voice broke through the sound of the gloves. "Tyler, I'm Brad. I'm a paramedic. Is it okay if we trade places? I'd like to see Luke."

"I don't want to leave him. I can't leave him," I begged. Suddenly, the urge to stay with him overpowered me. I couldn't move.

"I understand. I just need to be closer to help him, so I'd like to be able to stand right where you are standing. You can stand right next to me outside the car, but I need to trade places with you," he said to me, not forcefully but in an assertive tone.

"Okay. Okay," I said, trying not to take my eyes off of Luke.

"Why don't you slowly take a step outside of the front window. Watch your head as you come out."

Against all my instincts, I took one hand off of Luke. Then the other. And put my right foot outside the now wide-open front windshield. I placed my hand on the top of the dashboard to help keep my balance, but it slipped off from my hand being covered in blood.

I didn't realize just how much blood was on me until the lights from the trucks met my hand on the dashboard.

His blood was covering my hands to the point that I couldn't see my own skin. My long-sleeve shirt was now bright red up to my elbow and down my chest and stomach.

I was normally fine seeing blood, but this was Luke's blood.

This isn't good. Luke isn't okay.

I started to hyperventilate. *If this is all Luke's blood, then he's way worse than I thought.*

Turning my head back to Luke, I wanted to get back in the car and help.

I needed to help him.

The paramedic put his hands on my shoulders and turned my body back toward him.

"Tyler, I want you to look at me. Look at my face, okay?" he said.

I tried to look up to him. I couldn't focus. I needed to help Luke.

"Keep moving toward me. I'm going to hold your head so you don't hit anything or move your neck too much."

"Okay... but Luke..." I said, barely able to put words together.

"I know. The best thing you can do to help him is to

make your way out of the car so I can get in and take a look. Let's go. I'll help you out."

He then placed his hands on the sides of my head, guiding me out free of the bent car frame without putting too much stress on my neck and keeping me from hitting my head.

As soon as my left foot cleared the car, another firefighter swapped the paramedic's hands for his own and held my head straight while another put a support collar around my neck to keep my head in place.

During all this, the paramedic smoothly slipped inside the car, right where I had been standing a few seconds before.

"Luke? Can you hear me talking?" he said in a calm but sturdy voice.

I was starting to feel really dizzy and felt my body trying to lean forward. Two thick fireman-jacketed arms slid under my armpits from behind and helped hold me up.

"Tyler, how are you feeling? Do you know where you are right now?" the firefighter in front of me asked.

"I... I think..." I was struggling to put words together. I felt like I had earlier when I was trying to count Luke's heartbeats.

Like I was fading. Falling asleep.

No. NO.

"Tyler?"

"Tyler."

"Tttyyyyr."

"Ttttttttlllrrrr."

My eyes closed slowly, red, blue, and white flashing lights barely visible through my closed eyelids.

Silence.

Sometimes movies get things right.

The unconscious man slowly regains his faculties. He hears muffled noises, but stares into a black abyss. A soft white glow slowly starts to push away the inky black in slow bursts, but with a strange red hue.

Then sounds start to get more defined as he slowly regains the ability to open his eyes.

It was too bright.

There was beeping around him. Talking.

A bright fucking light right in his face.

Why was the light moving? Was he moving?

Wait… It was me.

I was waking up? Had I been asleep?

I couldn't turn my head. Why couldn't I turn my head?

"Ughh…Uhghh…Wuuhhh…? Wha…"

Why couldn't I speak?

"Ttttttlllrrrr."

"Tttyyyyr."

"Tyler."

"Tyler? Tyler, can you hear me?"

The light flashed one more time before it turned off for good, and I was staring up into the face of a stranger.

"Tyler, do you know where you are right now?"

"What?"

"Do you know where you are? Do you know what happened?"

"No, what?"

The stranger turned his head to talk to someone else. "Patient's alert, but we have an altered verbal GCS."

"What? What's GCS?"

"Tyler, you've been in an accident. You're in an ambulance right now and we are taking you to the hospital to make sure everything is all right. Do you remember anything?"

What? Shit. Shit. What happened…

"I… I think… I don't know."

"It's okay, just try to relax and breathe slowly through the mask."

"What's wrong with me? What happened?"

As the words came out, pain came rushing in through my right side like someone was stabbing me.

"*Fuck!*"

My whole body shook, but I seemed to be strapped down.

"Try to hold still. Breathe slowly. You were in a car accident and you broke a few of your ribs. But everything is under control and we are almost to the hospital to get you fixed up. You just passed out for a couple minutes there. I know it's really painful, but I want you to keep breathing slowly and deeply, okay?"

My heart was pounding.

What happened, what happened... Dinner. Sushi. A car... Luke... LUKE.

"*Luke!* Where's Luke? Where is my brother?"

"Luke is on his way to the hospital too. Now, please, Tyler, breathe slowly," he said in a calm voice.

How the fuck could he be calm?

I don't know how much time had passed, but the ambulance seemed to come to a stop and the guy sitting over me looked down toward my feet and started moving in that direction, low so his head didn't hit the roof.

"Okay, Tyler, let's get you inside."

Luke... Where is Luke?

Lauren sat there next to my bed holding my hand. They gave me something for the pain and I felt like I was managing things okay, but no one would tell me about Luke.

"Anything?" I asked desperately, knowing that she knew just as much as I did.

"Not yet. I'm so sorry. They won't tell me. We aren't family yet." Her voice was shaky, like she knew something bad was coming.

He'll be fine. It's Luke. He'll be fine.

I looked at Lauren. My throat was tense, and tears were starting to well up.

"I... He... It was really bad, Lauren... He looked... really bad."

She looked back at me with soft, caring eyes, but red, like I'm sure mine were from holding back tears but trying to look supportive and positive.

She just smiled at me, probably unsure of what to say back.

Through the checkered security glass of the treatment room, I could see my doctor working on some paperwork at the nurses' station. She was head down and writing with intense focus as a nurse on the other side of the counter used both hands to raise and turn her computer monitor on an extendable swing arm mount so my doctor could see what she was looking at.

The nurse had her left arm resting across her stomach, hand under her right armpit. Her right arm was bent sharply up so her right hand, gently curled into a fist, could rest on her lips.

Whatever was on the screen made my doctor put her pen down on the clipboard. She crossed both her arms across her chest as if to hold herself. Her hands, resting on the opposite biceps, gave a gentle but noticeable squeeze, making her scrubs wrinkle under the pressure.

When she looked back at the nurse, I could see her take an extremely slow and deep breath, chest raising her crossed arms with the deep inhale. As she exhaled, she raised her head and chin, looking to the bright fluorescent lights above her.

A few seconds later, another doctor, I assumed a surgeon due to the surgical cap still covering his head, came around the corner to speak with her. They chatted for an unbearable while, just barely visible to me from the corner that rounded the nurses' station.

Is this about Luke? What happened? Is that his doctor?

They said a few last things to each other, and I could see the surgeon look off to the left along the hallway they were standing in and take the same deep breath my doctor had just moments before. Before turning and walking in the direction of my room...

14

I was looking down at my feet. Black shoes on maroon carpet. Why did these places always have weird carpet colors?

My hands were out in front of me, forearms resting on the stained wooden surface meant to hold the weight of heavy, old books. My hands were in loose fists and resting together while my thumbs rubbed each other slowly from knuckle to nail, first my right thumb, then my left before repeating.

My right hand had a quiver. Not a full shake but a light quiver.

I was trying to breathe slowly through my nose to hide my true desire to drop my jaw, look skyward, and inhale all the oxygen in the room.

I felt like I was going to pass out. Was I not breathing enough? Was I just worried about what I had to do?

It didn't matter. I had to do it.

My hands flattened out, palms down, on the few pieces of paper I had brought up there with me. As I moved my hands wide and down to the edge of the slanted wood top, affixed to a sturdy base that hid my legs from the room, I read the first line I had written to myself before saying it aloud.

"I wasn't sure how I would start this. I've never done this before, and I hoped to have never needed to. I sat at my desk for countless hours, just staring at a blank page. I could have looked up examples online, or asked my family what they would have said first… But that wouldn't have been *from me.*"

Pausing for a second, I tried to take a slow and steady breath through my nose. My chest slowly quivered like my hand had been just moments before as the air made its way into my lungs.

"After a long while of repeatedly writing something down, crossing it out, crumpling up the paper, and throwing it on the ground, I had to take a step back and look at the paper-covered floor and slow down.

"I had to remember that this is just one of the millions of times I will talk about Luke after this day. I had to remember that there is no one perfect speech, no one perfect story, no one perfect description of Luke to give. There are millions of amazing, sad, hilarious, loving, and depressing stories I could tell, and will tell. But I can't tell them all here.

"I could tell you things you already know about him. About his amazing heart and his propensity to share it with everyone around him. But you already know that about him, or you wouldn't be sitting here listening to me.

"Here I will tell you about the Luke that I knew. One who was unique to me. The one no one except maybe a select few in this room would know. Only then will I do him justice by imparting something unique onto you to remember him by. Something that will make today mean more than just a common experience or shared perception."

I paused again to take a breath and slow things down. I knew that if I spoke too quickly, I'd start to choke up and cry.

I needed to be strong.

"Everyone in this room knows how much he meant to me. How much I relied on him growing up. We did everything together when we were kids.

"I should rephrase that… I did everything he did when we were kids."

I looked to the front row at my parents. I knew it would be a bad idea. If they were crying, it would make me cry. Starting at their feet, I moved my eyes upward.

They were sitting so close together they were attached from foot to shoulder. Both of their hands were holding each other's, resting on their adjoined thighs. Moving up to their faces, I saw smiles.

Smiles! I couldn't imagine what it would take for parents to smile in a situation like this.

My throat felt like old leather, nostrils flared, but I could sense my right cheek start to flex as a small grin appeared on my face to join them.

"He was successful at almost everything he tried to do, and he enjoyed everything he did, which is probably easier when you're good at everything. But he wasn't deterred when things didn't go his way.

"While everyone here knew this about him, you might have not seen him behind closed doors when things didn't work out so well. Since we played sports together, drove to school together, shared a bedroom in our earliest years, and hung out with friends together, I got to see Luke in all his glory and all his failures.

"I don't know who first said it, and I'm sure it's been said a million different ways, but the underlying message remains the same. 'Someone who wins all the time never learns how to lose. Show me someone who loses gracefully and with self-reflection, and I'll show you a winner.'

"Luke lost sometimes. In fact, probably just as much as the rest of us. But he didn't focus on the losses, which is why he always seemed to be so successful.

"There was a reason for this, how he was able to come out seemingly on top all the time...

"Legos."

A bit of laughter broke out in patches throughout the stuffy room, which gave me a few seconds to remember I was around people who were supportive. This gave me a bit more strength to keep going, with a small smile on my face.

"When I was learning how to count, Luke played this game with me. He would lay all the rectangular eight-by-two pegged bricks on the floor in a pile. They were all the colors that we had available to us after years of mixing different sets together into a massive storage trunk of loose pieces.

"He'd then pull out a couple six-sided dice.

"The goal of the game was to build the tallest tower possible before it fell over. Whoever's turn it was would pick two bricks up from the pile and roll both dice.

"If you rolled a four with one of them, Luke would hold up four fingers for me," I said as I lifted four fingers up in front of my face, visible to everyone in the room, "and he would tell me that the brick I add to the tower can only be connected with four of the pegs, leaving the remaining four sticking off to the side.

"I could pick which four pegs to use, and attach it in any configuration I wanted, but I could only use four."

Looking around the room at all of Luke's friends, I could see that everyone was listening intently with a smile, so I kept going.

"If I rolled a one with the second dice, my next brick could only be connected to the tower with one of the corners, leaving all the other seven pegs exposed and unsupported.

"Over time, the constant addition of randomly supported bricks would make the tower increasingly tall, unstable, and unshapely. Eventually, it would all come crashing down to the floor in a heap of pieces when gravity decided it wanted to play too."

I paused, thinking about all the times I looked down at the pile of bricks on the floor. Looking at what I thought had been strong but had fallen just the same.

"After I counted all the bricks that fell to see how far we'd gotten, Luke would let me use ten to build a base. Any configuration, and as many overlapping pegs as I wanted to use. Once that was built, we'd get back to rolling the dice and building up from the new base. With a sturdier foundation, the tower would get taller with the attempt before crashing down again.

"With each collapse, he'd let me add to the base. But instead of another ten, he'd only let me add nine. Then with the next collapse, only eight, and so on. The game could last for way longer than a child's attention span could handle, so we never got to zero before having to stop playing, but we got very close.

"It was so much fun to me as a little kid. I got to build something with Luke and it was always a challenge."

I looked down at the lectern, realizing that I was barely reading the papers in front of me and just telling the story from memory.

I took a deep breath, remembering that this next part was the hardest.

"This taught me so much about him, and about how he handled chaos and loss. No matter how much you try to build, things happen. It's about building that base stronger from the pieces that fell and trying again.

"As your base gets stronger, the tower gets taller, which makes the crashes more substantial. The crashes feel more real. But you still have more opportunities counting down to the last brick.

"This round, Luke made it to the end and had no more bricks to build up a base. Every other challenge in his life, every struggle, every battle...every moment of chaos...he had a few left to use, and he used them well and with confidence so that this time the tower would be the tallest.

"But this was his last round. His tower fell for the last time."

I was struggling to speak. My throat was solid now, tense from the pressure of holding back the heavy breaths and wanting to cry.

My eyes were now so watery that it was difficult to read.

"Losing Luke was a tower collapse for all of us, but I can hear him saying to me, 'This is not the end of your game; you still have bricks left for your base. Keep building. Eventually you will get to zero too, but today you still have a base to construct, dice to roll, a tower to build, and people close to you to play with."

15

Patient: Tyler Lawson, Male, Age 29.
Session: 1
Session Objective: New Patient Discovery Session
Primary Psychiatrist: Dr. Rachel Kittrell, M.D.
Recording Start: 14:32 8 January 2019

14:32:47 - Dr. Kittrell: *Hello, Tyler, it's nice to meet you in person.*

14:32:51 - Tyler Lawson: *Hi, yeah. You too.*

14:32:58 - Dr. Kittrell: *Please, have a seat. Anywhere you'd like. I hope you don't mind if I record our sessions. This helps me take notes and allows me to refer back to our conversations later.*

14:33:11 - Tyler Lawson: *Umm...*

14:33:16 - Dr. Kittrell: *You look a little uncomfortable. I totally understand that. One thing that I like to mention before we get started is that everything you say in here, everything we discuss is entirely confidential. And that includes these recordings. To protect your privacy, I am legally and ethically bound to never discuss anything outside of this room without your permission. The only situations where that changes are if I feel there is an imminent threat to your well-being or someone else's, or if you divulge that you intend on committing a crime. Even if we run into each other at the supermarket, I won't approach you or say anything unless you come to me first... Total anonymity.*

14:33:52 - Tyler Lawson: *Okay...*

14:34:01 - Dr. Kittrell: *When I go home, there is very little that I can even discuss with my husband. These conversations never leave this room. When my husband asks me how my day was, or if there was anything interesting that happened, all I can say is "Good" and "Yup." It's actually great because we can have conversations without it always being about work... We can talk about our kid's school activities, the new restaurant down the street... and why, after all these years of being married to a fan, I still don't understand football.*

14:34:31 - Tyler Lawson: *Hah... okay... I guess it's fine.*

14:34:47 - Dr. Kittrell: *Thank you. I really like it because I can focus on what you're saying, and I don't miss anything due to frantically scribbling it all down on a notepad. You can have my full attention.*

14:34:59 - Dr. Kittrell: *Have you ever been to see a counselor before? Or have you had any experience with therapy?*

14:35:21 - Tyler Lawson: *No... I guess my fiancée has been to counseling before. She was the one who talked me into calling... But no, I haven't before.*

14:35:42 - Dr. Kittrell: *That's good... I know it can be a little uncomfortable at first, but I promise it's temporary.*

When I first meet new patients, I like to discuss my methodology and how I like to go about things... as well as discuss a bit of what you'd like to get out of our sessions. Every counselor goes about it a little differently, and every patient is different. So, the most important thing before we begin... to me... is to make sure that we are on the same page for some basic things like... one... the most important question... What would you like to get out of our conversations?

14:36:14 - Tyler Lawson: *I... I don't know. I guess... I guess I've been having a hard time recently. I've been having trouble sleeping and focusing... I guess I'd like to feel a little better and get back to normal, I guess.*

14:36:51 - Dr. Kittrell: *Okay, that's a good start. Have you tried any medication to help you sleep? Like, from your primary care physician, or anything else on your own?*

14:37:07 - Tyler Lawson: *No, not really. I guess I don't like the idea of medication. I don't feel like I should need it… I'm not a fan of hiding the symptoms. I'd rather fix the problem instead. I guess it's why I was hesitant to come here. I didn't want to just sit down, tell a story, and get pills.*

14:37:38 - Dr. Kittrell: *I'm glad you said that. Thanks for explaining. That actually fits right into my normal practice. I'm a psychiatrist, so I can and do prescribe medications from time to time, but I don't do it as much as you'd think, and not for all my patients... and I actually like it to be more of a last resort.*

What I like to do is some psychoanalysis first to see if your situation falls into one of three things. Sometimes it falls outside of these, there are a lot of unique situations and I always adjust, but a lot of times it's one of the three. Sometimes medication is important to help correct natural imbalances or to help with permanent or persistent issues. That can be conditions like bipolar disorder or schizophrenia on the extreme side or minor things like ADHD. These are things that don't necessarily improve with normal conversational therapies and require a bit more help to control.

The second situation is when medication can help open someone up to therapy, or to help suppress behaviors or thoughts that are interfering with conversational treatments. It's almost always a temporary situation where a patient is only on something for a few months or a few years, but can ultimately be taken off the medication when they develop the mechanisms to combat the underlying causes of the condition. I actually see this a lot. This is very common to help with things like depression and anxiety. But I should add that I never start with the medication. I only prescribe it after I get to know the patient more and I feel that it will help their long-term well-being. I don't prescribe to patients who aren't in some form of a recurring treatment program to ensure that they are always working toward the goal of getting better, and not just getting a pill to hide the symptoms, as you put it.

The third situation is when a patient and I both feel like they are progressing through counseling successfully, without those other distractions getting in the way. This is also very common and makes up a lot of the patients that I see on a regular basis. Everyone can benefit from talking to an impartial third party, and oftentimes that's all they needed.

Does that help answer your concerns about medication? Do you have any questions about that?

14:39:56 - Tyler Lawson: *No, that makes sense.*

14:40:03 - Dr. Kittrell: *Good. Okay... back to my question from earlier... What would you like to get out of treatment?*

14:40:22 - Tyler Lawson: *Well... a few months ago, my brother passed away...*

14:40:33 - Dr. Kittrell: *I'm so sorry to hear that. Were you close?*

14:40:42 - Tyler Lawson: *Yeah. We were... It was hard.*

14:40:52 - Dr. Kittrell: *Did you have difficulty sleeping before he passed away? Or is it somewhat of a recent issue?*

14:41:11 - Tyler Lawson: *It's... well... I guess it's been a problem for a while.*

14:41:20 - Dr. Kittrell: *Earlier you said that your fiancée... what is her name?...*

14:41:26 - Tyler Lawson: *Lauren.*

14:41:29 - Dr. Kittrell: *Lauren... That's a beautiful name. Thanks. You said that Lauren talked you into coming to speak with me?*

170

14:41:43 - Tyler Lawson: *Yeah.*

14:41:49 - Dr. Kittrell: *Was that connected to your brother passing?*

14:42:08 - Tyler Lawson: *No... Maybe... I don't know... I've just been having a hard time. She thought it would help.*

14:42:21 - Dr. Kittrell: *She sounds like she cares a lot about you. Now... other than difficulty sleeping, what do you mean when you said you were having a hard time?*

14:42:38 - Tyler Lawson: *I don't know... Everything just seems harder... It's harder to get out of bed... which I'm sure is from not sleeping well... but... I just have a hard time doing things.*

14:43:11 - Dr. Kittrell: *What kinds of things?*

14:43:21 - Tyler Lawson: *I don't know... Things... Normal things. I just don't want to do normal things anymore... Like go to a restaurant... or wash my car.*

14:43:46 - Dr. Kittrell: *How do you feel when you try to do them? What's different now?*

14:43:58 - Tyler Lawson: *I'm just... tired.*

Patient: Tyler Lawson, Male, Age 29.
Session: 4
Session Objective: Outpatient Psychotherapy - Diagnosis Confirmation
Primary Psychiatrist: Dr. Rachel Kittrell, M.D.
Recording Start: 14:03 17 January 2019

....

14:35:27 - Dr. Kittrell: *I noticed something last session and just now that I wanted to ask you about. I noticed you are looking around the room a lot. From the bookshelves to the carpet and up to the ceiling. Is there anything in particular you are looking at or thinking about?*

14:35:42 - Tyler Lawson: *Yeah, sorry... I do that...*

14:35:51 - Dr. Kittrell: *Don't be sorry. There is nothing wrong.*

14:36:00 - Tyler Lawson: *I guess... it's just something I do...*

14:36:09 - Dr. Kittrell: *Can you describe what you're doing? What you are thinking about as you look around?*

14:36:15 - Tyler Lawson: *I... I just like to know my surroundings. I need to know all about them.*

14:36:24 - Dr. Kittrell: *What do you need to know? Anything in particular?*

172

14:36:33 - Tyler Lawson: *I've done it since I was a little kid... I just need to understand things around me... I don't know... It sounds weird when I say it that way.*

14:36:45 - Dr. Kittrell: *It doesn't sound weird to me. This is a new environment for you. It's normal to look around and be curious.*

14:37:01 - Tyler Lawson: *It's not that. It's just... how I think.*

14:37:09 - Dr. Kittrell: *How do you think?*

14:37:17 - Tyler Lawson: *I guess... I just need to focus on something and dissect it.*

14:37:27 - Dr. Kittrell: *What do you mean by dissect? Can you walk me through an example? I saw you looking at the carpet over there to your left a lot. What were you thinking about when you were looking there last session? Do you remember?*

14:37:43 - Tyler Lawson: *Well... It started by just looking at the pattern. I noticed a few loops of the threads weren't aligned perfectly like the rest of the ones next to it...*

14:37:55 - Dr. Kittrell: *Did that bother you? That they weren't aligned?*

14:38:08 - Tyler Lawson: *No... yeah... well, a little. It just got me thinking about why*

173

they were out of alignment. I was thinking maybe... maybe there was a chair there in the past and the weight pressing down on it creased the thread... or maybe it's a cheaper carpet and some machine mis-wove on a stitching pass... or... I don't know... This is making me sound crazy.

14:38:37 - Dr. Kittrell: *Not at all. What you're describing is actually very common. When some people are in unfamiliar or uncomfortable environments, they often try to distract themselves. Sometimes feeling anxious about something causes our brains to look around for things it can try to understand and release some of the pressure it's feeling... Were you feeling anxious?*

14:39:02 - Tyler Lawson: *No... I wasn't scared. It's just something I do.*

14:39:09 - Dr. Kittrell: *Anxiety and fear are different emotions. They can coincide sometimes, but I'm curious... Why did you say 'scared?'*

14:39:19 - Tyler Lawson: *I guess... I thought anxiety was from being afraid of something and being nervous because of it... right? I wasn't afraid... just uncomfortable.*

14:39:31 - Dr. Kittrell: *Sometimes. But it's entirely possible to be anxious but not fearful... Anxiety is about experiencing or predicting discomfort and expending a* lot of psychological and emotional effort to maintain control… or some level of comfort. I didn't get a sense that you were afraid, but were you feeling uncomfortable?

14:39:56 - Tyler Lawson: *I guess… yeah.*

14:40:01 - Dr. Kittrell: *Why?*

14:40:06 - Tyler Lawson: *I… I… I didn't like the idea of getting counseling.*

14:40:13 - Dr. Kittrell: *Any particular reason? Don't worry, you won't hurt my feelings. You can be honest.*

14:40:29 - Tyler Lawson: *I guess… I guess I always felt like you had to be broken to see a psychiatrist. Or a psychologist… or whatever. I guess I just was feeling like… like maybe I was broken to be in this room… It made me uncomfortable.*

14:40:48 - Dr. Kittrell: *Do you think you're broken?*

14:40:52 - Tyler Lawson: *No… I just… I didn't like the idea of possibly needing professional help.*

14:41:03 - Dr. Kittrell: *When do you feel like professional help is needed?*

14:41:11 - Tyler Lawson: *Like what you were saying about people who had conditions* that couldn't be fixed without medication... like... like schizophrenics... not normal people... not like... situational stuff.

14:41:29 - Dr. Kittrell: *Situational things can be pretty substantial for a lot of people. How do you feel about when people are depressed? That can sometimes be situational but can also have a pretty severe long-term impact on someone's life.*

14:41:48 - Tyler Lawson: *I... I mean... I don't know... I guess... I guess when I've been depressed, it kind of goes away... eventually... but I didn't feel... 'broken' or anything... just that I was feeling bad.*

14:42:02 - Dr. Kittrell: *Do you feel depressed often?*

14:42:09 - Tyler Lawson: *Sometimes... But it's usually just from being tired. I just don't want to do things sometimes... and if I spend too much time in my head, I don't feel great.*

14:42:27 - Dr. Kittrell: *Have you ever thought about hurting yourself?*

14:42:33 - Tyler Lawson: *I hate that question.*

14:42:39 - Dr. Kittrell: *Why? Have you been asked it before?*

14:42:46 - Tyler Lawson: *I... I just feel like people don't want the real answer... Like they just ask because they have to.*

14:42:59 - Dr. Kittrell: *What do you mean?*

14:43:04 - Tyler Lawson: *Like... what are they going to do with the answer? No one wants to hear... yes... or something. Like... what are they going to do with that information? I just feel like most people say no. It's just easier.*

14:43:28 - Dr. Kittrell: *Is it easier for you?*

14:43:33 - Tyler Lawson: *I see what you did there... Smooth.*

14:43:40 - Dr. Kittrell: *Hey, I tried. But you still haven't answered the question. Have you?*

14:43:51 - Tyler Lawson: *No... Not really.*

14:44:00 - Dr. Kittrell: *What do you mean, 'not really?'*

14:44:09 - Tyler Lawson: *I... When... when I'm really tired, or frustrated... I guess I just think... I think... I wouldn't care if it just... stopped... It's not what you think...*

14:44:31 - Dr. Kittrell: *What do I think?*

14:44:36 - Tyler Lawson: *I don't mean 'stopped' like... that.*

14:44:42 - Dr. Kittrell: *How do you mean it?*

14:44:50 - Tyler Lawson: *Like... like a nap... like... like everything can just... stop... for a while.*

14:44:59 - Dr. Kittrell: *What do you mean by stop? Do you have any examples?*

14:45:09 - Tyler Lawson: *Like drifting in space... I don't know... It's hard to describe... Like silence... Like... if something's so bad... the feeling that would be there when it's just done, or you don't have to deal with it anymore... like you don't have to do anything... It's just over... It's silent.*

14:45:33 - Dr. Kittrell: *Do you like the silence? Let me rephrase that... Do you like the idea of silence?*

14:45:42 - Tyler Lawson: *I... I think so. It just sounds... peaceful.*

Patient: Tyler Lawson, Male, Age 29.
Session: 11
Session Objective: Outpatient Psychotherapy - Major Depressive Disorder, General Anxiety Disorder.
Primary Psychiatrist: Dr. Rachel Kittrell, M.D.
Recording Start: 13:02 14 February 2019

....

13:15:47 - Dr. Kittrell: *If it's okay with you, I'd like to discuss some medication options. Some recurring themes I notice in the conversations we've had over the last several weeks make me think that you might benefit from something that could help to reduce your general anxiety… By doing that, you should be able to sleep a little better and it may help with a few other things like your overall treatment progress. What do you think?*

13:16:16 - Tyler Lawson: *I don't know… How would anxiety medication help me sleep? Why that instead of sleeping pills? I don't want sleeping pills. I don't want to sleepwalk or anything like that… I hear that happens a lot.*

Tyler adjusted himself in the bucket leather chair from leaning on his right side to his left, visibly uneasy. His hands were in his lap, fingers interlocked as his thumbs nervously rubbed up against each other.

The idea of medication made him feel like he didn't have control over himself.

13:16:32 - Dr. Kittrell: *Based on what I've heard, I think that your difficulty sleeping has to do with how you process the day you've had and how you pre-process the day you're going to wake up to. Medication that's solely geared toward helping you sleep treats the symptoms of the problem, not necessarily the root cause...*

Remembering back to the first session they had about medication philosophy, Tyler was glad that this was her reasoning. The last thing he wanted was to develop a pill-popping... dependency... Not that people taking sleep meds were addicts. He simply felt that if you needed medication to do the normal things in life, like sleeping, you were doing something wrong.

He was still apprehensive about the idea, still felt... uncomfortable. Looking down at the floor between them, the carpet weaves catching his focus, he hesitantly responded.

13:16:54 - Tyler Lawson: *Okay, I guess that makes sense...*

There was no real coordinated thought that popped into his head as he looked at the floor. He didn't really know what he was supposed to think about. How did he feel about going on medication? How was he supposed to feel about it?

Dr. Kittrell was looking a little more intently at Tyler now. Her head cocked at an angle as she dipped her chin down and looked up softly toward him with a slightly raised brow.

13:17:08 - Dr. Kittrell: *You look a little apprehensive about the idea. Is there something you're concerned about?*

Tyler took a few seconds before responding, thinking hard about the question.

13:17:22 - Tyler Lawson: *How long do you think I'll need to be on it?*

He didn't know why that mattered, but he asked anyway. Perhaps it was a need to differentiate between needing a lifelong crutch or a short-term splint?

Why did it matter?

He didn't know.

It mattered to him.

13:17:33 - Dr. Kittrell: *Well... it depends on the results we see. Sometimes it's just for a few months to get back to a normal rhythm. That partnered with counseling can do a lot of good. Sometimes, it can be for a few years, or longer...*

Tyler winced at the last comment.

He tried to play it cool, but Dr. Kittrell noticed...

13:17:51 - Dr. Kittrell: *Does that worry you? I know... A few years can seem frustrating, especially for those who are a bit apprehensive about medication in general...*

Not sure how to respond, he just sat there. It did bother him, but he trusted her. She didn't seem like the kind of doctor to just prescribe and call it a day. She'd said as much, but saying and doing were different things.

Even though he trusted her, this whole conversation still made him feel...broken.

13:18:08 - Tyler Lawson: *How can you tell the difference between short-term or long-term needs? Like... do you do periodic reviews or something?*

13:18:22 - Dr. Kittrell: *These types of medications can take two or three months before they start showing results. They need to build up in your system slowly. So, what I typically do is give it a bit of a chance to take effect, then do periodic reviews of whether or not it has the desired result...*

13:18:46 - Tyler Lawson: *Okay...*

Noticing Tyler's discomfort, she continued, not waiting for a longer response from him. She hoped that with more explanations of the process, he'd feel more at ease. After all, she really believed this would help him, and she really wanted to help him.

He was clearly a good kid and he wanted to get better but needed to get out of his own head. He needed to take a step back in order to process things better. If she could help him reduce his anxiety, she knew he could respond to psychotherapy in an even more positive way in the long term.

Without it, she didn't feel he was developing the coping mechanisms he needed to handle his depression.

13:18:55 - Dr. Kittrell: *During those periodic reviews, I check to see if it's making a positive impact on what it was selected to treat. If not, we review other options like dosage adjustments, a different medication, or eliminate it altogether. It just depends on the results.*

This sounded like she was throwing darts at a wall. Were these meds really that unpredictable?

Tyler was looking at her face now, making occasional eye contact to show that he was focusing. This was hard for him to do. He always felt weird locking eyes. So, he looked away every five or so seconds as she spoke to seem like he wasn't staring.

13:19:17 - Tyler Lawson: *So, I'd have to be on something for months before we'd even know if it works?*

It was a little unsettling to him, the thought of playing trial and error with medication that altered your brain...

13:19:27 - Dr. Kittrell: *The medication I'd like to try is called an SSRI, which stands for selective serotonin reuptake inhibitor. It's commonly used for anxiety and depression. These medications have a few different classes. SSRIs are on one end of the spectrum, and the usual process involves starting with one class, evaluating its effectiveness, and moving down the line. But yes, it takes a little while before they build up enough in your system and show an impact.*

13:19:58 - Tyler Lawson: *That sounds like roulette...*

13:20:03 - Dr. Kittrell: *It can seem like that. The reasoning is that everyone is different when it comes to neurobiology and metabolisms. It isn't quite like chest pain from clogged arteries visible in medical imaging where you know to use vasodilators to open up the veins and let blood flow more freely. Sometimes, the signs and symptoms of psychological conditions don't entirely indicate which specific imbalance needs to be adjusted, and there isn't a dot on an MRI pointing us in the right direction... So, we make an educated decision as a starting point, give it a trial run, then reevaluate. Does that make sense?*

It did, but it still sounded like a gamble. The idea of being a lab rat to find something that worked made Tyler feel worse in an already frustrating situation. He didn't like the idea of psychiatric medications, let alone guessing at what should be a more reliable process.

13:20:45 - Tyler Lawson: *It does, but I don't like it, to be honest. Is there some blood test we can do to see what works?*

13:20:56 - Dr. Kittrell: *There is one that can sometimes help indicate treatments based on C-reactive protein levels, but it's extremely expensive due to it being so new, and it isn't covered by most insurance... and to be honest, it's potentially only slightly more accurate than the current process. If you have a ton of money lying around, it's something we can look into. But in my opinion, it isn't reliable yet.*

13:21:26 - Tyler Lawson: *Okay.*

13:21:31 - Dr. Kittrell: *One thing that has surfaced is that there is a strong genetic component to how our bodies process these kinds of medications. There is a strong connection between medications that work for multiple people within the same family. So, what I usually ask is whether or not you have a family member who has taken anti-anxiety medication or antidepressants in the past. If there was something that worked for them, it has a good chance that it can work for you as well. Has anyone in your family been on any medications like this?*

Tyler couldn't think of anyone who took medication like this in his family. His father definitely didn't. He was from a "grin and bear it" generation.

His mom? Maybe.

13:22:06 - Tyler Lawson: *I don't think so... I don't know... I doubt it.*

13:22:18 - Dr. Kittrell: *Would you be comfortable asking them? I know it can feel a little uncomfortable. But given how concerned you are about medication in general, I think it could be pretty helpful to reduce the trial-and-error period.*

13:22:34 - Tyler Lawson: *Okay... I'll ask my mom if she knows.*

13:22:41 - Dr. Kittrell: *Sounds great.*

Patient: Tyler Lawson, Male, Age 29.
Session: 12
Session Objective: Outpatient Psychotherapy - Major Depressive Disorder, General Anxiety Disorder.
Primary Psychiatrist: Dr. Rachel Kittrell, M.D.
Recording Start: 14:03 19 February 2019

Tyler walked into the well-lit office and took a seat in his normal chair, opposite Dr. Kittrell. The room had a bit of an antique feel to it, with patterned area rugs trying to hide the boring standard office carpet underneath. There was a large floor-to-ceiling window behind him, which would have had a great view, being on the fourth floor, but it was unfortunately directly facing a parking lot packed with office park visitors.

Dr. Kittrell had a unique way of starting sessions. She didn't like to start things off or ask her patients specific questions. She wanted them to sit down and just... start. Saying the first thing that came to mind, or something they were thinking about discussing ahead of time was a better way of picking a conversation path than a more... prescribed conversation.

Most times, Tyler would have to sit there for a few seconds in silence, her gentle facial expression saying to him without speaking, "And...?"

The first few sessions were awkward. Tyler stumbled around what to talk about first. If he said one thing, would she ask why he picked it? If he said another, would it set them on a path that was a waste of time and ultimately money?

He didn't know.

He obsessed about what to say first before every session.

Not once did she ask him why he picked a topic, nor did he feel like a topic was unproductive. Nevertheless, he obsessed.

But today was different. He obsessed, but for a different reason.

He knew exactly what he needed to talk about but was still feeling apprehensive.

Tyler was wearing a hooded sweatshirt with a nice big pocket in the front. One that was through and through to either end. The kind you could put your hands in and they could sit comfortably resting on each other in the warm comfort of the soft and empty pouch.

His hands were resting in the pocket like they always were. It usually felt relaxing to him. He didn't have to hold his arms up. He could just rest them against the bottom of the pocket and relax his muscles.

But today his arms weren't relaxed, and the pocket wasn't empty.

His right hand was wrapped around a small bottle. He was twisting it slowly in his fingers, feeling the paper sticker that was wrapped around most of it and the smooth plastic that was everywhere the sticker was not.

The lid was smooth on the top but had a grooved edge to grip with a small tab that was used to remove it.

He twisted the bottle more, feeling like he might slowly remove the sticker on it by friction.

Dr. Kittrell sat quietly, patiently, waiting for him to start talking. She knew it wasn't productive to try and rush him, and she could see that he was deeply upset about what he was going to say to her.

She knew to let him speak in his own time.

14:04:08 - Tyler Lawson: *I saw my parents this weekend... I drove out to their house for dinner on Saturday.*

14:04:16 - Dr. Kittrell: *Yeah? How was it?*

She asked him casually, knowing full well that it would not have a casual answer. The hesitation he was showing had her a little nervous about what he would say next. She could see he was in pain.

But from what? She didn't know yet. She wanted him to tell her, desperately. She would never show or say it to maintain professional distance, but she cared deeply.

Doctors were supposed to maintain a professional emotional distance from their patients. Oftentimes, it was easier said than done. She'd become a psychiatrist to help people. When you had that motivation, you inevitably felt more invested in your patients than if it were purely a medical relationship.

Where other medical fields allowed a doctor to have more time between visits, and the visits themselves were more transactional than conversational, it was possible to do a better job of maintaining professional separation. Psychotherapy could make that separation difficult.

With psychotherapy, a doctor got to know someone. Really *know* someone. Sometimes, patients told their counselor things they'd never tell a spouse or a parent. With that kind of visibility into a person's inner workings and emotional state, a person got more… invested.

14:04:22 - Tyler Lawson: *I asked them about medications… They hadn't been on anything before… but…*

Tyler continued to fumble around with the tiny container in his pocket. He was struggling with his words. It was difficult to say what he wanted to say.

He pulled the container out of his pocket and into the well-lit room, the sunlight making the orange translucent plastic glow and transmit an orange hue onto his thigh.

Twisting it slowly until the paper sticker on the outside of the bottle was facing him, he started to read it in his head silently…

RX: 739456
QTY: 60
Date Filled: 4/17/16

Tyler's eyes struggled to read the first line on the sticker. He could see it in a blur at the corner of his vision as he read the rest, but he struggled to go back to the top and look at it.

After a few seconds of staring at the orange plastic, he looked up to the top and read the first line out loud.

14:04:56 - Tyler Lawson: *Luke Lawson… Bupropion… 300mg…*

He held back tears, feeling them well up in his eyes. His throat was starting to tighten up….

Tyler stood up from his chair slowly and took the two steps across the patterned rug toward Dr. Kittrell and handed the pill bottle to her. His hand was slightly shaking, and he recoiled his arm as soon as she took the bottle from him and put it back into his sweatshirt pocket.

He knew she saw it shaking, but it still felt safer to hide it in the sweatshirt, his other hand grasping it, trying to hold it still as he made his way back to his chair.

He sat down with his arms firmly in the sweatshirt pocket. Tense. Silent. Waiting.

Dr. Kittrell removed her glasses from the hard case she had on the end table next to her chair, which also held a box of tissues and a notepad. After putting them on, she lifted the bottle up and read it to herself silently and slowly.

She had heard what the medication was when Tyler said it out loud. But out of respect, she took the time to read it to herself quietly. She didn't want to just push it back in his direction as if the bottle had no meaning.

It meant a lot to Tyler.

When she was done reading, she looked up in Tyler's direction and smiled with a soft, genuine caring look.

She stood up and walked to Tyler, handing the prescription bottle back to him before returning to her chair.

Tyler looked at the bottle again and put it back into his pocket, his right hand firmly grasping it.

14:05:31 - Dr. Kittrell: *How do you feel, knowing that Luke was on an antidepressant?*

Tyler's whole face was tense. He was trying desperately to hold back tears, but one made its way out and slowly slid down the left side of his face.

With the bottle firmly in his right hand, he pulled his left out of his pocket and quickly wiped it off his cheek and took a quick, wet sniff in through his nose to keep it from running.

Dr. Kittrell stood up again and brought a fresh tissue box to the end table next to Tyler's chair before sitting back down in hers.

14:05:58 - Tyler Lawson: *He never told me… I… I didn't know.*

Dr. Kittrell's eyes began to turn red as she struggled to hold back her own emotions and focus on her patient.

14:06:05 - Dr. Kittrell: *Why do you think he didn't tell you?*

Tyler sat there, silently. Thinking. He took another deep sniff in before reaching to the tissue box she had set there for him and rubbing a tissue gently below his nose.

14:06:22 - Dr. Kittrell: *He seemed to care about you immensely. You two were really close and shared a lot. That's a big thing to hold in.*

14:06:35 - Tyler Lawson: *My mom said that he was having a hard time the last few years… I always thought he was fine… I don't… I don't know why he hid this from me.*

Dr. Kittrell could see the deep pain in his eyes. The brother he loved and felt closer to than anyone else in this world… had a secret.

She knew that he might not know why Luke didn't tell him, but she knew that this was something that could really help his outlook on treatment in general. If he knew that the person he saw as strong and together was getting treatment on the side, it might help Tyler be open to the same.

14:06:50 - Dr. Kittrell: *How do you feel about your own treatment, knowing that Luke was going down a very similar path?*

14:07:02 - Tyler Lawson: *I… I don't know. I guess… I guess a little better.*

Tyler used the crumpled tissue he had in his hand to dab at his nose again. His eyes were watering, but he just let it happen. He didn't care.

14:07:22 - Tyler Lawson: *I… But… I feel like I failed him twice.*

14:07:30 - Dr. Kittrell: *What do you mean?*

14:07:38 - Tyler Lawson: *I... I should have been able to see him like this and try to help him...*

14:07:45 - Dr. Kittrell: *Sometimes, it's very hard to see these things unless someone lets you in. He might have been trying to help and protect you.*

14:07:57 - Tyler Lawson: *I... I guess.*

14:08:06 - Dr. Kittrell: *What did you mean by twice? What was the other time that you felt you weren't there for Luke?*

14:08:20 - Tyler Lawson: *I... I was there... but I couldn't help... The car accident.*

This was the first time Tyler had spoken about that situation and how he felt. It was an important moment to talk about it, but it was clearly causing a significant amount of pain.

14:08:31 - Dr. Kittrell: *What do you mean, you couldn't help? From what I read in the police report you showed me, you did everything you possibly could have.*

14:08:40 - Tyler Lawson: *I... I was a trained EMT... I should have been able to save him. I tried... I tried...*

Tyler was crying now. Struggling to put words together. This had been weighing on him for a long time now. He needed to say it out loud.

14:08:56 - Tyler Lawson: *If I'd have done better, he might still be alive. I failed him twice… I just… I wasn't ready for it.*

14:09:09 - Dr. Kittrell: *No one is really ready for something like that. Why do you feel like you could have?*

14:09:17 - Tyler Lawson: *For YEARS I obsessed about things like that, running through car accident scenarios in my head. Since EMT school I couldn't help it. I had to be prepared. I practiced and practiced in my head. I ran through that stuff all the time. Why didn't it work then?*

14:09:31 - Dr. Kittrell: *Sometimes, no matter how hard we prepare, the situations we are in can throw us something new. And judging by his injuries, there was no way you could have saved him unless you were a surgeon and had an ER right next to you. Sometimes, we are put in impossible situations. No matter how hard you practice in your head, the real situation will be different. That's not your fault. In those situations, you do what you can, when you can. And that's all we can do. From everything I know, I'd say you did everything you could for him.*

Tyler didn't know how to respond. He just sat there, tears streaming down his face.

14:09:54 - Dr. Kittrell: *It will probably be a while before you forgive yourself, but you're human. Luke was human. And humans aren't immortal. When horrible accidents like this happen, we are often left to try to make sense of it all, and feeling guilty for surviving or not feeling like we did enough to prevent it all is perfectly normal. But it will go away with time.*

14:10:17 - Tyler Lawson: *Why should it go away? I don't know if I want it to.*

Dr. Kittrell knew that this particular type of guilt would take some time to heal. She wasn't going to solve it in this session but would have to work on it slowly over time.

He might not want to face it completely now, but they would get there. Slowly.

14:10:24 - Dr. Kittrell: *How would you feel if I were to put you on the same medication that Luke was on? Bupropion is a little different than the SSRI that I was recommending last session... but knowing that it might have been working for Luke makes it a great place to start.*

Tyler sat there for a few seconds trying to collect himself and think about what Dr. Kittrell just said.

He hated the idea of medication. But if... But if Luke had taken something to help him, maybe it was okay for him to do the same.

Sometimes, the people you thought had everything together needed help too.

This was a side of Luke he'd had no clue existed.

He looked up directly at Dr. Kittrell, making strong eye contact.

14:10:35 - Tyler Lawson: *Okay...let's do it.*

16

"**Y**ou're smiling," she exclaimed, cracking a smile of her own. She had to think back hard to when the last time it was that she'd seen him smile.

She couldn't come up with anything. Not even when Tyler was talking about his wedding. He loved Lauren, there was no question. But it was too soon after losing Luke and it took a little while for the medication to take hold.

The anxiety and depression were really interfering with how he saw himself, his family, his life, and his future.

He was just, as he put it, tired.

Therapy isn't often a happy ordeal for people to go through. So, it was a refreshing thing to see. It was a reminder that progress did come, sometimes very slowly, but it did come along.

"Ha, yeah. I guess I am smiling," Tyler said, looking up at Dr. Kittrell.

After a few moments of silence, she took the hint. He wanted her to ask.

"Well? Let it out!"

"Lauren's… Lauren's pregnant," he said, trying to maintain composure. Trying to maintain his cool.

"Really? That's fantastic! Congratulations!"

"Thanks." Still trying to stay cool, he sat still, but the smile was undeniable.

"How do you feel about it? Are you excited?" she asked. He looked reserved about something. She could tell that he was happy, but something was still there. Something was keeping him from expressing it outright.

"Yes... Of course! Good. Great," he said, looking up and smiling. Smiling for so long now that his cheeks were starting to heat up from the muscle strain.

"And...?" she asked, trying to goad him into some sort of deeper answer.

"I... I just wonder... I hope that I'm ready." He paused to look back up.

"Am I ready?" Tyler asked, with genuine curiosity.

"What makes you think you aren't ready?" Dr. Kittrell asked, hoping he'd explain a bit more. Every new parent was nervous about being responsible for a new life. But with Tyler, it was likely something different, something more... specific.

"I don't know. I think that I'm ready to have kids. I mean, I'm old enough and we've been married for a little while. But..." He paused again.

"Yes?" she asked intently.

"I think about all the parents I know—mine, my friends, you know... and I just don't know if I have it all... together... enough for me to be responsible for raising another person."

Dr. Kittrell gave him a second to add to that, but he just sat there, waiting for an answer.

"What makes you think that all those other parents had everything together? Remember a few months back when we were talking about public perceptions?"

Tyler nodded.

"Well, public perceptions are just that. Public. Behind closed doors, I'd bet every one of them had a mini panic of their own. What was the analogy we used?"

She had to think about it for a few seconds, looking up and off to the corner of the room as she racked hard through all the conversations they'd had.

"Ah, yes. Comparing everyone's highlight reel to your bloopers."

"Yeah, I remember that. But…" He paused, trying to figure out how to word this. It was a real concern; it kept him up at night. As real as it was, it was still difficult to put it into words. "I really think a lot about this. What happens when he or she's a teenager? What happens when they need a rock-steady guide to handling things?"

"What kind of things?" she asked.

"Well, things like high school dating or struggles or… I don't know. I just don't feel like I have that stuff really figured out yet."

He paused, still thinking about how to communicate this.

"Like, what do I say when they are depressed? Or something. I feel like they'd need some sturdy figure to help guide them."

"Why don't you feel you'd be able to be that figure?"

"I don't know. I think that going to counseling means that I didn't know how to navigate that stuff," he said, with genuine concern on his face now, slowly replacing the smile that was there moments before.

"I disagree," she said firmly, looking right into his eyes.

"What?"

"I think that you going to counseling means you know exactly what to do. You struggled, you had hardship, you felt like you were stuck. But you did something about it. You asked for help."

Tyler sat there silently, looking down at the floor. He was confused.

"But I didn't. Lauren pushed me to come here."

"Yes, but that's because you surround yourself with people who care about you. People who helped point you in the right direction. And not just that, but you acted on the advice they gave you."

He was still sitting there, absorbing what she was saying.

"You walked into my office over twelve months ago, anxious, depressed, and uncomfortable. Today you sat down with a bright smile on your face. The only way you got there was because you took this whole process seriously. You wanted to get better, and you did what you needed to do to get better. You might have not been willing to admit it at the start, but the fact that you were so dedicated and receptive to this whole process means that you did."

She waited for that to sink in a little before she continued.

"Today, you sat down and told me about how you want to be the person who can help your child be a stronger person. Not unlike Lauren, who helped point you in the right direction, you want to be the one to point, the one to help your child navigate life. Isn't that what parenting is about?"

"I... I guess. But I don't know if I'll know where to point."

"Look, no one knows how to handle everything. People who say they do are lying. True strength and stability is knowing when you have answers and knowing when you need to ask for help. People who pretend to always have the answer never learn how to seek answers to new problems. They try to convince themselves that they know what they are doing. That does not mean that they actually do."

Tyler was looking up at her now. This was the most she had said to him outside of asking questions in a long time.

"If I were a child, I'd want to have parents who listened, empathized, and worked hard to help me find the right answers compared to parents who pretended to have it all figured out.

"Tyler, you have an inquisitive mind and caring demeanor. If you ask me, that's all you need to be ready."

17

Tyler grabbed the plastic tub and flipped it over, spilling all the Lego bricks onto the carpeted floor. There were maybe two hundred pieces in there, and they were all strewn about in front of them. He used his hands to scoop them into a pile before pulling out a couple dice from his shirt pocket. He didn't think he'd need the dice yet, but he brought them out of habit.

"Are you ready?" he asked before putting down a book to use as a hard surface.

"Now, what you have to do is use a few pieces to make the bottom... like this," he said as he started to connect the bricks into a square pattern that would hopefully be strong enough to support a small tower.

Lauren was standing in the kitchen, peering around the corner quietly so as to not let them know she was watching.

"Okay... now... what we do is roll the dice and add two new pieces to the top."

Two small hands reached out and grabbed the closest pieces and held them in a firm grip, brown eyes now looking up at Tyler.

The small right hand carried the trapped blue rectangular brick up to an awaiting and equally small mouth to coat it with a fair amount of saliva.

Tyler reached down to grab the small wrist and pry the plastic toy piece from his mouth.

In a soft and patient voice, he said, "No... not like that."

With Tyler's hands on top of the now slimy fingers wrapped around the blue brick, he helped to guide them to place it on top of the awaiting base. He pressed down with gentle but firm pressure until the brick sat securely in its new home.

"There. Like that."

Lauren felt a small tear well up under her right eye. Watching them play this together was making her immensely happy. Tyler had been talking about it for what felt like as long as she'd known him.

"Okay now, let's do the next one. Are you ready, Luke?"

He was still too young to respond with coherent words, but the smile and big eyes aimed up toward Dad told him all he needed to know.

"Yeah? Okay, let's build a tower."